Matzo Match

A LESBIAN AGE GAP ROMANCE

ROZ ALEXANDER

Also By Roz:

"Hot for the Holidays Series"

Matzo Match

Higher

A Masc for Purim

"Steamy Shabbat Shorts" (Amazon Exclusives)

Bring Me Home

Light My Candles

For MEA—my forever co-host.

Note From Roz:

This story is about two Jewish lesbians. This entire series (*Hot for the Holidays*) is about queer Jewish people falling in love and having hot, explicit sex. Sex in Judaism is celebrated, is a *mitzvah* (a good deed/a commandment), is divine. These stories are meant to honor and uplift Jewish love (including interfaith love), and also to be lovingly honest and hopeful about the modern Jewish community.

And mostly I wanted to write some gay, Jewish smut.

The Jewish community includes people who identify with all races, genders, sexualities, abilities, as well as a wide spectrum of beliefs and practices. There's no one "right" way to be or do Jewish—and the absence of an identity or belief here is not a condemnation on my part.

Judaism is a religion of joy. I hope Sam and Jordan's story brings you some.

This story contains: alcohol, angst, eating, emotional abuse (past), explicit sex, mentions of fertility struggles and pregnancy (minor characters), penetration, racism (offscreen), toxic relationship (past), sex toys, and, as always, an HEA (Happily Ever After)

If any of that doesn't fit what you want/need out of a story right now, this might not be the one for you.

B'Simcha (in joy),
Roz

Glossary & Passover 101:

Note: because many of these words are translated and/or transliterated, there are multiple accepted spellings. These are also the simplest definitions and if you're interested, I encourage you to dig deeper into each!

Afikomen – based on the Greek word for dessert, is a broken piece of matzo that we play hide and seek with on Passover.

Ashkenazi – Jews who are from, directly or indirectly, Eastern European countries

Charoset – a paste, or chunky mixture, made of fruits and nuts and served on Passover

Haggadot (the plural of **haggadah**, which means "telling" in Hebrew) are the books that are used to drive the seder – there are hundreds of haggadot, all unique.

Haleq – the Persian version of charoset

Hebrew – Semitic language spoken by multiple Jewish communities

Ladino – Romance language spoken by some Sephardic Jews

Nowruz – the Persian new year, celebrated by Persians, Jewish and otherwise

Passover is an eight (for some, seven) day festival commemorating Jewish freedom from persecution in Egypt. Passover **sederim** (the plural of **seder**) typically take place the first one or two nights of the holiday.

Seder literally means "order" in Hebrew, and they get a bad reputation for being long, boring, hungry events of rote storytelling. But sederim are what you make of them, and some are raucous celebrations of freedom and a commitment to justice in the modern era.

Seder plate – a ritual plate that displays many symbolic foods used in the seder

Sephardic – Jews who are descended from the Jewish populations that left Spain and Portugal in the late 15th century

Yiddish – Germanic language spoken by some Ashkenazi Jews

Chapter One

"What're you hosting this year?" Virginia yelled over the children arguing somewhere in her background. "I mean, what night?"

Sam, standing in her kitchen talking on the pastel pink corded wall unit, peeling carrots for an overnight stew, pulled the phone away from her ear for a particularly loud bout of fighting. "Gin, why are the girls so upset? It sounds like there are ten of them, not just two!"

"Oh, who can keep track? I mean, really? I think Yael did something to Gabi's doll, but honestly, who can know? Anyway, I'm asking about Passover because, normally, you've already sent out invitations by now, and Ben is trying to figure things out with his parents. They want first night."

"Shoot, I can only really host a first night seder. I promised Cara and T I'd go to theirs for second night—they're hosting two, but this is their first year as a couple, and their guest list is massive. So they already put me down for second night. *And* Cara threatened me with being dropped to the second tier of invitees next year if I back out."

"That's fine!" Virginia turned away from the phone to

bargain with the girls for a few moments of quiet. "Honestly, it might be nice to have an adults-only seder for once. And I can't go with Ben and the girls anyway because I'm on call the next day. So, why don't I just come alone?"

"One, 'adults only' definitely sounds like I'm throwing an orgy for Passover." At this, Virginia made a sound like that wasn't such a bad idea. Sam ignored her and continued. "And, two, I want to see the girls." Sam had been spending at least part of every Jewish holiday with the Patterson-Tells for the last five years. She couldn't imagine not having the girls running around her house, tearing apart her decorscapes while looking for the *afikomen*.

"Well." Gin paused for a moment while considering the options and, Sam thought with awe, probably doing some incredible mom thing simultaneously. Every call with Virginia was a master class in multitasking. "What if Ben and I host last night? Like a send-off seder?"

"Do people do that?" Sam wondered aloud while she began to peel the last carrot.

"Who cares! Probably. I figure three seders are better than two. I mean, I should be getting serious Jewish points right now for even suggesting it."

Sam laughed. Virginia wasn't Jewish. She'd been raised in the Mennonite faith and decided not to convert when marrying Ben. Regardless, she lived a very Jewish life with Ben and their children. Sam had once told her, as a joke, that she should be awarded "Jewish points" for all of her above-and-beyond holiday spirit. Virginia had never let her forget about that and had teased her about it ever since.

"Fine, sounds like a plan to me. And, I'm sorry, by the way, for not planning sooner. It's just that, well, it's the first year since—" Sam stopped, cut off by a lump in her throat and a loss of words.

Virginia's voice was softer when she responded. "I know,

honey. But it's time you put that jerk in the past. Start building out some of your own traditions."

"You're right." Sam took a deep breath and bit violently into the carrot in her hand as if she could cut right through her sadness with her molars. And why couldn't she? It was almost spring! Anything was possible! "It is time! And I know Passover is just the *longest* holiday, but I do love it so much. It'll be good to host." Sam nodded affirmingly to herself, the headset almost slipping from between her shoulder and ear. "I'll invite Alyssa and Leo over. Oh, and I promised I'd invite my neighbor, though I doubt he'll come. I'll see if anybody else needs somewhere to be. Do you have anyone who needs a spot?"

"No, it seems like everyone is sorted." Then, with a bit too much enthusiasm in her voice, she asked, "but what about a plus one for you?"

"Vir-gin-ia!" Sam shouted each syllable of her name separately, "I literally can't bring myself to say her name yet. You know damn well I haven't been looking for any sort of date."

Virginia laughed, a loud, wild sound. "Okay, okay! You sound like my granny saying my name that way. Fine, it'll be the normal group, we'll have a great time, I'm sure. I've got to run and get these creatures of mine to bed, but I'll let Ben know about our last night seder plan, and you let me know if you want me over next week to track down all the crumbs."

Sam rolled her eyes at her best friend's characterization of cleaning out the chametz, an often neglected, if not totally forgotten, part of the holiday tradition in her home, but said, "You know I do."

Chapter Two

Sam shot out of bed seconds after her alarm began playing its latest Pop Top 100 selection, pulled on the first clothes she found, and left her apartment an hour before she'd normally leave for work to run as fast as she could to the grocery store. The whole way, she imagined she'd make it there before any other customers if the empty streets indicated anything.

Still, she found herself chanting, "Please still have matzo, please still have matzo, please still have matzo," under her breath. It was only a few days away from night one of Passover, and she was way, way, way behind. So behind that, when her mother had called her the night before to just chat and casually asked how the preparation was going, Sam had stifled a whimper of shame.

Luckily, Virginia was coming over that evening after work to help her clean, including getting rid of all of the leavened bread products in her house. Sam thought she could probably convince her to do some light crafting too. Decor was at least 90% of why Sam loved to host, and she wouldn't skimp on it this year just because she was way off her timeline. It thrilled her to set a table with carefully coordinated table mats, dishes on top of larger dishes, delicate wine glasses—all set around floral arrangements and origami and paper cuttings. Candles! She needed some more candles too.

Most of all, she needed matzo. She could not believe she'd let it get so close to Passover without securing at least ten boxes of the holiday's tasteless, flat bread. *Fool!* Not only did she need two boxes for her matzo toffee crackle she'd serve after her own seder, she needed two more boxes for the crackle she planned to bring to Cara and T's. Plus, it was all she'd eat for the next week—matzo with eggs for breakfast, matzo pizza for lunch, matzo ball soup for dinner—until she was so sick of it, she'd be happy to not see it again for a year.

She arrived before the store even opened, so she took the time to stretch her legs and hips, her muscles happily humming from the run. *Thank you, weather,* she thought, so tired of having to run indoors on a treadmill. Breathing deeply and lifting her arms high overhead, she worked on calming her pounding heart. Once she felt a stillness settle over her, she took a seat on the nearby bus bench. Folding her arms over her chest, she realized she'd left everything but her credit card and keys at home. Somehow, she'd also managed to put on two different sneakers in her haste to get out the door.

Great, just perfect, she inwardly groaned, but desperate to hold onto the post-sprint peace, she forced herself to take in the beautiful, crisp day.

It was an early day of spring, and looking up at the tiny green buds on the tree overhanging the bus stop nearly brought tears of joy to her eyes despite all of that morning's stress. This had always been a big part of why she loved Passover so much. Even when she was a kid—and her siblings would whine and bargain to get out of sitting through the full Passover experience—Sam had loved that it felt like a way of welcoming in the freedom and history of her people *and* of the world around them. She made a mental note to make sure she bought a lot of flowers to decorate around the seder plates this year.

Look at me, Ms. Positivity over here, Sam wondered to herself. *And*, she continued, *honestly, if I can manage to get these thoughts back on track, maybe it is time to start thinking about Pauline.* Sam knew Virginia wasn't wrong, that she'd have to move on sometime. And it's spring! Love was basically perfuming the air.

Sam had been staring so intensely up at the tree in deep thought that she hadn't realized someone was now standing quite close to her. Her heart gave a little jump as she spotted them out of the corner of her eye, and she realized it was one of the sexiest people she'd ever seen.

The stranger had short hair, cropped down to stubble on the sides and back, and started to go salt-and-pepper on the side closest to Sam. Their crisp white button-up was tucked into dark jeans over camel-colored work boots. They were tall and leaning in profile to Sam against the bus sign pole, looking so at ease that Sam worried they'd actually been there before.

Had they witnessed Sam's frantic dash to the storefront, her ridiculous attempt to yank open a clearly locked door, and, most embarrassing of all, her luxuriating in post-run pleasure?

No, she felt confident she would have noticed someone so blazing hot even in her matzo-less distress. Especially someone who wore jeans like they were painted onto their body, the outline of a slim wallet clearly visible in the butch's back pocket.

Sam realized she was staring at this stranger's tight, denim-clad ass at the same moment she realized the stranger was looking at her with amusement. The stranger's eyes were a rich brown, just a few shades darker than their skin. Their full lips curved wickedly up at the corners and startled a tiny but audible gasp out of Sam.

The sound seemed to stoke their amusement, their smile widening to reveal blindingly white teeth.

Sam felt flames lick up from her chest to turn her pale neck and cheeks scarlet. Her rib cage now a furnace of mortification, Sam was convinced she was visibly sweating far more than she had on her run. She immediately jumped up, gripping her keys hard in one hand, and fled to the now open grocery store's front doors.

Sam was freshly out of the shower, still wringing her hair in a towel, when the doorbell buzzed. After a long day at work where her mind kept drifting back to the mortifying experience of the stranger catching her stare—plus the memory of the butch's taut body heating her up—she'd needed to let the cold water settle her system.

She opened the door to Virginia's splotchy, tear-stained face.

"Gin, what's wrong?" Sam could remember very few times in the last ten years when her friend had looked quite as distraught. "Did something happen to the girls?"

Virginia moved past her into the house, throwing her oversized crossbody purse onto the lime green armchair that illuminated the closest corner.

"No! No, they're okay. And luckily, they weren't there for it."

"For what? Are *you* okay? Did something happen to Ben?" Sam realized her voice was edging on shrill, but she couldn't help but be deeply concerned.

"We're all okay. It was just—" Virginia trailed off for a

moment, rubbing a hand over the side of her face. "Well, this woman at the Jewish middle school we're hoping to get the girls into, the admissions counselor, she assumed that I was Jewish, because I'm white, and that Ben wasn't, or that he'd converted, or something."

"Oh, Virginia." Sam's voice filled with so much sadness that the other woman put her hand up to stop her, knowing she'd start to cry again if Sam comforted her.

"And it was just this horrible mess. I got so angry. Ben has to deal with that kind of racism all of the time. As if he isn't facing enough as a Black man out in the world every single day, part of his own Jewish community suggesting he was an outsider really got to me. I wanted to shake her. Every time this happens, it's just as crushing."

Gin slumped down onto the gray couch that faced the entryway and put her head in her hands. "And it went wrong in a totally different way when I overcorrected and pointed out that I'm just white, which has nothing to do with whether or not I'm a Jew. For that matter, I am not Jewish. I did a lot of rude pointing." Virginia reenacted the angry pointing for Sam's benefit, coming close to poking Sam in the eye. "Then that horrible woman started questioning the legitimacy of my daughters' right to attend the program."

At this, Virginia took a deep breath and then suddenly laughed, the tension draining from her face. "And so Ben is the one who's all angry now, defending my honor, calling her a bigot and small-minded. I think he said something really Hallmark-y like 'interfaith relationships make the world beautiful.' The two of us, such a pair! Anyway, we left immediately and laugh-cried all the way to the car. Even if either of us still wanted to send our kids there, there's no way they'd let them in now."

"I'm so glad you two have each other." Sam reached over

and squeezed Virginia's hand, her best friend squeezed right back.

"Me too. He's just the best man."

"It's truly the school's loss. Those kids are for real geniuses. What are you two going to do about finding another place, though?"

"Oh, we'll figure it out. It's not the only Jewish school in the area, and I think we both actually want to send the girls to public school. So maybe we'll just enroll them in a Jewish after-school program. I'm not convinced any of these private schools understand a single thing about race. And I'm not sending my kids anywhere that doesn't have Black teachers anyway."

She took another deep breath and let go of Sam's hand. They fell comfortably into conversation for a while about Michael, the racial competency therapist Virginia had been seeing since before the girls were born, and Michael's new haircut and clothing, and whether that meant Michael was finally dating again. And that led to both of them telling the week's work horror stories, which included tell of Sam's boss "accidentally" screen sharing a photo of her new boyfriend shirtless on the beach. Then, somehow, they drifted into the latest episode of their shared favorite reality show: The Great British Knitting Program.

"Enough small talk! We're not here for chit-chat. We're here for serious Passover business: the cleaning of the crumbs." Virginia announced in a great vocal impersonation of Sam's mother, who was known to walk away from any conversation she deemed unimportant or small.

Gin continued the impression by popping up and exaggerating a march into the kitchen. Sam rolled her eyes and followed her in through the archway.

"Okay," Sam said, settling down into a chair at the kitchen table and picking up her bright pink scissors. "I thought we could ease into the holiday spirit with some crafting."

Virginia held the back of the chair opposite Sam and leaned forward, squinting at the paper scattered across the table. "Crafts. Of course you think that's easier than cleaning. How about I wipe down the counters while you craft? Feed two birds with one seed and all that."

"Fine, but you're really missing out."

Virginia made a noise in the back of her throat that suggested she very much disagreed before pulling out all of the cleaning supplies and getting to work on the counters.

Sam put on her springtime playlist, and they worked in relative quiet for a while before Virginia looked over at her quizzically.

"So, what are you cutting out over there?"

"I'm making construction paper napkin holders. I told you, I want to do everything that Pauline always thought was ridiculous this year. Let my craft flag fly!" Sam focused on a tiny bit of paper she was steering her scissors around.

"First, major points for saying Pauline's name without weeping. Second, I can see they're napkin rings. I mean, what are these decorations you're so carefully cutting out?"

"Oh, matzo." There was a beat of silence as Dolly Parton lamented to Jolene about infidelity in the background, and Samantha realized Virginia had stopped her relentless stovetop scrubbing. "What?"

"You're making custom paper napkin rings, and the decoration on them is just going to be tiny tan squares? Do you hear how that sounds?"

"Virginia! Do you have no faith in me?"

"I do, but, honey, matzo are just beige squares. They're not known for their sex appeal."

"Everyone will be delighted by them, just you wait. Very sexy napkin decor will be delivered." At that, they both laughed, and Virginia declared her wrists needed a break from crumb-hunting.

"Is this how you did it with your parents?" She asked Sam while picking up a small paper matzo for inspection.

Sam gently smacked it out of her hand., "The crafting?"

"Well, sure, but I meant the chametz cleansing."

"Ah, I see. Crafting wasn't really a family activity. That's something I picked up as a teen." She swept all of the craft bits away from Virginia's seat with her arm. "And the cleaning was way more intense."

"How so?"

"My parents were really observant when I was growing up. We'd all spend a full day right before Passover cleaning and scrubbing. Then we'd cover the countertops and appliances in foil."

"Like, aluminum foil? Like Reynold's wrap?"

"Yeah, but store brand."

"Why?"

"I don't really know. In case we'd missed any crumbs, I think. Maybe?" She paused while trimming a particularly delicate bit of the napkin ring. "I'll have to ask my mom. I was pretty young when they eased up on some of that stuff."

"Was it because they had your sister and brother? I can't imagine doing all of this with multiple kids."

"You *have* multiple kids, and you're over here doing it with me, your oversized third child."

"You're not a child, except when you're being a big baby about losing at trivia. And it's honestly easier cleaning someone else's house. Plus, you'll return the favor next week."

"Can't wait." Sam's voice made it clear that she could, in fact, absolutely wait.

"Great! So, what about your parents?"

"Well, we moved away from our Jewish community so my mom could get a better job. And it just seemed like my parents found the stuff they actually thought was meaningful instead of the exact traditions their own parents had done. So, like, one year, we burned all of our chametz in the fire pit out back the morning before Passover started, and we talked about Moses every night for a week. And then the next year, I sold all of our bread products to a Christian neighbor, but there was no big bonfire, and we started only observing one night of Passover."

"Do you miss some of it?"

"I miss a lot of it, actually. I find our traditions so rich in history and symbolism. I feel like I'm always looking for an excuse to pick up more. I mean, before Pauline, I was getting really into Shabbat—" Sam stacked all of her matzo squares delicately atop each other.

"Oh yeah! I remember that. You were dating that pottery teacher, Candace? Candy?"

"Claris."

"Claris! And she made you those candleholders just for your Shabbat candles! They were so cute. I really thought she was the one." Virginia's hands mimed what Sam imagined was supposed to be small, cute candle holders, though the gesture looked a lot more like Gin was trying to pinch her cheeks.

"I truly cannot believe you remember that, but yes, she did. And I still have them. They're in the box with all the other stuff I put away because Pauline thought it was all tacky. I've never met someone who was so at odds with their own identity before."

"This is more than I've heard you talk about her since the break-up. Are you missing her?" Virginia made an elaborate show of looking very ordinary, calm, and neutral. Sam rolled her eyes at her in response.

"No, actually, I think I've recently totally stopped missing her." Sam could hear the surprise in her own voice. "I still feel really burned by the end of everything, though. I don't know when I'll actually heal from that, but I don't think about her that much anymore. Which, obviously, is awesome."

"So glad to hear it because my little sister just told me there's this new lesbian app—"

"No! Gin, I'm stopping you right there. I told you, I'm just not ready to start the whole getting to know someone, deciding if I trust them, investing time in a stranger thing."

"Okay, but—"

"Absolutely not. I'll meet someone casually. I don't know, however the young people are doing that now, at a bar, a work conference, at the—" She realized she almost said *grocery store*, thinking about the hot butch with the hot butt from that morning. She felt her face turn red, and Virginia raised an eyebrow. "No! No. I need, like, a spring fling before I start planting bulbs."

"Well, it's spring now! Fling away, use the app, make your bio something like 'clear out my cobwebs, and I'll return the favor.' You know, classy." Virginia made an obscene face.

"I cannot believe you're a mother."

"Those girls are lucky such a comedian decided to give birth!"

"Fair enough, but I want the next person I meet to be real. I met Pauline through you, and obviously that didn't turn out the way I wanted it to, but it felt good to meet someone in person."

"Ugh, truly the worst thing I've ever done."

"What? Introduce me to Pauline?"

"Yes! What a jerk."

"If that's the worst thing you've ever done, you might be eligible for sainthood. Do Quakers have saints?"

"Mennonites, Sam! And no, we don't. That's like a Catholic thing. Maybe Lutherans have saints too."

"And Mormons."

"Do they?"

"Aren't they called, like, the Church of Latter Day Saints?"

"You are just trying to distract me from my mission of getting you on this app."

"Yes, I am," Sam said as she finished cutting out the last matzo square. "Because I am not interested, like, at all."

"Honey." Virginia seemed to be gathering herself for round two of persuasion, but then she saw the look on Sam's face. "Okay. Just remember that Gabi and Yael's babysitting years are numbered."

"Wow, so I'm not just looking for a wife, I'm looking for the other mother of my unborn children, huh?"

"Yes! Low pressure for a fling."

"I'm not even planning on having kids, Gin. Find someone else to matchmake."

"Dogs need babysitters too! Find the mother of your future dog children."

Sam flicked a crumpled-up ball of construction paper at Virginia, and they both dissolved into laughter.

Chapter Four

The day leading into Passover went past twice as fast as Sam
felt it should have. She'd been so busy at work that week that
there'd been very little time to prepare at all. She felt a rush of
gratitude for Virginia when she realized how essential her post-
work, mid-week clean had been. So, now, even though she was
an hour behind on all of the cooking—and had just realized
she'd used up all of the matzo to make dessert, which was definitely, certainly, absolutely not because she'd eaten an entire
tray of the chocolatey matzo by herself and then had to
remake it—her house was pretty clean, and the table was really
freaking cute.

Beyond her self-satisfaction at the table setting, however,
she could sense a sinking grief, which was partially what had
led to eating fistfuls of dessert in the first place. This was the
first real event she was hosting after her split with Pauline. But
she shoved that down. No time for surprise weeping when
there was soup to finish and salmon to bake. *Get it together,
Sam! You have to feed these people.*

As she shoved the last plate of chocolate matzo toffee into
the fridge to set and cool, Sam fished her phone out of her

pocket. "Can you come early??? Matzo emergency!! Need moral support as I ... make matzo?!" She texted Virginia.

It was less than a minute later when the return question came, "Be there in under 1 hr! Can I bring my guest early too?"

"Her guest?" Sam wondered aloud to her kitchen as she started the dishes. Maybe a fellow midwife. She just wrote back, "as long as they help too."

Her corded kitchen phone rang as she set her cell phone back down, and she nestled it against her neck as she started chopping apples for the charoset. "Hello?"

"Hey, it's Ben."

"Oh, hey! I was just texting your wife."

"About how handsome and witty I am and how sad you are that I'm not going to be there tonight?"

"Um, exactly, yes."

"I mean, who will bring the fun now?"

"Well, it *is* Passover, so I'm not sure how much fun we should be having."

"True enough. So, I was hoping I would get your answering machine-"

"Oh, you don't even want to talk to me! You want to leave one of your horrible dad jokes on my machine."

"Listen, you're the one who insists on living in the past. I at least make it interesting."

"Mhm."

"No, I was calling to thank you, and gratitude should live on forever. But if I have to say it to you: Thanks for sending those flowers over to me and Gin, and no, I don't want you to go punch that admissions woman."

"I'm surprised the flower shop actually wrote that on the card."

"Oh, they did. I actually cried from laughter. I've never seen such a mixture of florals and aggression before."

"I mean, do you even know me?"

They both laughed, and Ben asked how the prep was going in a voice that suggested he knew she was tremendously behind, which led to Sam telling him to go fly a kite but also to hug the girls for her.

* * *

Forty-five minutes later, she heard the buzzer as she was straight-ironing her last curl into submission. She yanked the plug out of the wall, checked her makeup quickly—good enough!—and scurried to the door.

"Oh, thank g—" Sam began as she took in her best friend. Virginia stood centered in front of the door, a hunter green pantsuit standing out starkly against her creamy skin, a wine bottle in each hand. Sam stopped short as she looked over Virginia's shoulder and spotted the top of a cropped head of salt and pepper hair. Definitely not Ben's beautiful curls, and none of the midwives or doulas Virginia had previously intro-duced her to. "Uh, hi, Gin and..." She trailed off and waved a questioning hand in the direction of the person who was half-buried in a sleek light brown leather backpack, rooting around and utterly unphased by meeting someone new.

"Hi, Sam! Happy Passover. Here's some wine." Virginia brandished the two bottles at her friend. "This is Jordan, my good friend. You've heard me mention Jordan before, right? My good friend? She's great. You'll love her."

With that, the stranger looked up, straight into Sam's eyes, and both of them stopped breathing.

Sam felt a moment of sheer panic and didn't even bother to question why Virginia was being so odd. Jordan's rich brown eyes went wide, then softened into thin lines and a blindingly white smile. She stuck a hand out.

Oh shit.

"Nice to meet you, Sam."

Samantha hesitated a minute before meeting her palm with her own. "Welcome, Jordan."

And with that, Sam let the hot butch from the bus stop into her apartment.

* * *

"So, we're here to make matzo?" Jordan asked, placing her backpack on a chair in the living room and slipping off her shiny brown leather high-top sneakers.

"Yep. Yes. Yeah, matzo. I ran out, made some miscalculations on how much I needed for everything." Sam typically would have made a joke about how comfortable Jordan seemed in her space, but her heart was still racing from the sheer serendipity of this person having reentered her life after such a casual and embarrassing encounter. Instead, she put the wine down on the entryway table, busied herself taking Virginia's light coat and purse, and even started leaning down to take Gin's shoes until her friend laughed and lightly shoved her away.

"I've never made matzo before," Jordan continued casually, ignoring that Virginia had backed away from Sam's fussing, and now the host had picked up and put down the wine bottles three times. "Do you know how?"

Taking a deep breath to recenter herself and internally chanting *get it together,* Sam nodded, shook her head, and headed to the kitchen to put the wine in the freezer. "Let me get these on some ice."

"Was that a yes or no?" Virginia asked, following her through the archway. "And one of those bottles is pinot noir."

"Well, I like to chill my red wine," Sam said nonsensically. Gin knew Sam only drank white wine.

"I do, too," Jordan added, and Sam glanced over at her, catching the butch woman's honeyed smile.

"That's very nice for you both, but I brought it for me, and that's weird. Sam doesn't even drink red wine." Virginia pulled the bottle from her friend's hands and walked it over to the table. "Weirdo."

Jordan shot Sam another charming grin before following the wine to the table. She picked up one of the cloth napkins, stroking a finger along the edge of one of the homemade napkin rings. "Matzo rings. These are so cute."

Virginia twisted the cork out of her wine bottle and plunked it down in front of her seat. "Sam made them."

"Wow, you're talented." Jordan touched it gently again, looking up from under lowered brows, and Sam felt her stomach drop. While this stranger was checking out her crafting skills, Sam checked her out. She was even better than Sam remembered from shamelessly ogling her in the early morning sunlight. Jordan had come dressed in well-fitted gray slacks, a dark floral bomber jacket over a well-pressed off-white button-up. When she bent her neck to look at the papercraft once more, a gold chain tucked under her shirt shifted on her tan neck. So the hot butch had a name, was real, was *in her kitchen*.

Shame and desire and confusion warmed her in equal measure. Sam cleared her throat.

"Thanks, Gin helped."

"I really did not. In fact, I mocked her for making them, but they are cute." Gin clapped her hands and put on a serious face. "Ok, honey, sacred matzo making time! How do we go about doing this?"

Sam proceeded to teach them all the straightforward recipe and baking method. Jordan continued to look totally at home in the kitchen in a way that equally unsettled Sam and turned her on. This stranger was clearly flirting with her, and

Sam seemed to have forgotten how to flirt entirely. Virginia cracked jokes at each step in the baking process and kept shooting immature, suggestive looks at Samantha behind Jordan's back. Sam concentrated on getting the bread done in time, sounding as normal as possible, and attempting to cool her face covertly on the now-cold wine bottle.

* * *

Alyssa, Leo, and Carly showed up together more than ten minutes early. Alyssa and Leo owned a condo near Carly and Joanna's apartment in a gayborhood on the northside, and they'd decided to carpool. Sam felt her heart glow when she heard this. Two years prior, Alyssa and Leo had been her ex's friends. Sam had never managed to be friends with a white, straight man before. Still, Leo had immediately won her over with his kindness and dorky sense of humor. And Carly and Joanna had been her friends for almost a decade.

Now, not only were they close friends with each other, but here they were at *her* first night seder. She often tried to be less petty, but boy was she glad to have kept their friends after the breakup.

"We're sorry to be so early," Alyssa said, kissing Sam's cheek as her twists fell forward and tickled Sam's skin. "I got nervous that if we didn't leave as soon as the babysitter showed up, then we'd never be able to leave."

As she moved past Sam into the house, Leo too leaned forward to kiss Sam's cheek. "Chag sameach. Thanks for making this an adults-only situation, pal. We have just about five hundred Passover events with the kids this week, and I just want one night of too much wine to myself."

"You should thank Virginia." Sam laughed as she ushered Leo into the house. "Oh, but also, will the two of you talk to her tonight about where your kids go? She and Ben had to deal with some real racist shit at one of the schools they were looking at, and I'm sure she'd appreciate any advice you have."

Alyssa's face fell, and she reached out to squeeze Sam's upper arm for a second. "Of course. Is Ben here? I should check on him."

"He's not, but you could text. He's at his parents' with the kids. Gin's on-call tomorrow, so she had to stay in town."

"Ok, I'll do that then." Alyssa nodded before taking a deep breath, and a smile returned to her face. "*Really* can't wait to dream about liberation at this dinner now."

Carly waited until Alyssa had turned to go the rest of the way into the house before wrapping her arms around Sam. "Before you even ask, no, Joanna didn't flake. She has a migraine."

"I would never call your wife a flake, Carly." Sam laughed into Carly's hair, returning her short friend's hug.

"It would be fair if you did. I think she even has that in her work bio." They both laughed and released one another.

"I'm loving this sweater! Where did this come from?" Sam smoothed her hands over Carly's arms to take in the soft wool some more.

"Of course you do. You're always like a walking rainbow." The sweater was made of rich gem tones woven together into stacked lines of varying lengths, and it felt like a good dream spun into yarn. "My ma sent it from this artist she loves back home in Oaxaca."

"Well, as I've said before, any time your mother wants to adopt me, I'll take it."

They walked into the apartment together, extolling Mama Jimenez's many virtues, when Sam remembered she'd left Jordan at the stove. "Oh, shit."

"What?" Carly asked, but then they rounded the corner into the eat-in kitchen, and Carly said, "Oh my god. 'Oh, shit' is right. Who is this hottie?"

Sam was confident Jordan had heard because Carly had made no effort to lower her voice. Still, the impeccably groomed butch just continued telling an animated story to Alyssa and Leo, who were clutching each other in laughter. Gin was taking what seemed to be the final matzo out of the oven with an amused smile on her face. Alyssa shot a raised eyebrow in Sam's direction, who stepped into the center of the room as Jordan delivered her punchline.

"Everyone, this is Jordan." Sam realized she'd automatically reached out and rested her hand on the other woman's arm before her brain could register how weird that was. *What are you doing, Sam?* She internally berated herself but left her hand there as she said, "Jordan, this is everyone. Well, that's not true. Carly's—this is Carly." Sam indicated her beautifully-sweatered friend with an open palm. "Carly's wife Joanna stayed home. You seem to have already met Alyssa and Leo."

Sam looked at Jordan, who was watching her closely. Jordan kept her rich brown eyes on Sam as she reached up and grasped Sam's fingers, pulling them off of her sleeve and placing them into her other palm. Then, while twining her fingers between Sam's, she reached her other hand out to shake with each of the new arrivals. Sam's brain seemed to fill with fireworks, followed by confusion, and then entirely short-circuited for a moment.

"So nice to meet you all," Jordan said in her deep, silky voice.

Sam felt her face go scarlet as she reminded herself she had just met this woman. She looked over her shoulder to see Virginia standing at the oven, mouth totally agape, staring at their clasped hands. Sam, wondering if she could die from blushing, faked a cough and pulled her hand from Jordan's to cover her mouth.

"Yes, Jordan is Gin's friend, er, guest. She came early to help me make matzo so we'd have enough for tonight."

"Homemade matzo!" Alyssa laughed, "Of course, you would do something like that."

"Plenty of people make matzo! Plus, there were only like two boxes when I finally made it to the store—"

"Jordan, do you know that Sam can never remember to go grocery shopping on time? Once, for Hanukkah—" Carly started before catching Sam's glare.

"Carly! No one wants to hear that horrible story. Yes, I can be a little forgetful when it comes to shopping."

"Carly, please, tell me over dinner. I can't wait to hear," Jordan faux-whispered, shooting Sam a wink that lit her up from the inside.

"Well, now, we can all get seated." Sam caught herself when she started reaching out to touch Jordan's back to direct her toward the table. Instead, she tucked her hands into the pockets of her dress. "Jordan, you can take Joanna's seat. I mean, your names are so close, we can just pretend the name card already says 'Jordan.'"

Jordan glanced over at her and winked again before moving to find her seat. Sam turned and caught Virginia's arm before her best friend could move past her to the table. "You have a lot of explaining to do, missy."

Virginia cackled and then suddenly wrapped her arms around Sam's shoulders. "I love seeing you get nervous. You deserve some stomach butterflies."

"I hate you."

"You're welcome."

It was at that moment that Sam realized putting Jordan in Joanna's chair meant she'd be sitting right next to her.

Sam stood behind her chair for as long as possible, explaining the run of the show to her guests. She'd assigned them each a reading from the cobbled-together haggadah she'd printed copies of and placed at their seats. "The theme of tonight is freedom through environmental justice. I've assigned you each a part, written on the back of your name card. So, Jordan, I guess you'll also do Joanna's part, which, if I remember correctly, is about environmental racism."

"Awesome," Jordan said, and Sam cut her eyes over to the stranger expecting to find a sarcastic look, but Jordan was looking enthusiastically through her haggadah for her parts. *Well, that's good then.*

Finally, once everyone had poured their first glass of wine and Sam had checked too many times to make sure they all had water, she sat. Immediately her leg bumped Jordan's, giving the hot guest another excuse to shoot her a wink.

Damn, this woman is sure of herself, Sam thought in awe. Yet she found that she was pulled in by Jordan's confidence instead of feeling annoyed. A self-assuredness that shone through the reading of the haggadah. Even her goofy old man Moses voice was appealing. The second time Sam was late in remembering to read her line about freedom from narrow places, it occurred to her that she was really in trouble.

Finally, it was time for dipping the bitter herb. Sam had been kind and put boiled potato on the plates for everyone instead of the usual vegetable. Once the ceremonial dipping and bites were taken, she stood up and announced she'd prepared some hors d'oeuvres for them to snack on and recharge before the rest of the reading. Jordan asked where the restroom was, and as she left the room, Sam let out a breath she didn't know she'd been holding.

Chapter Five

"So, Virginia, my dearest love."

Virginia tensed for a moment, wine glass halfway to her lips, eyes slowly sliding over to meet Sam's narrow stare. "Yes, my best friend in the whole world?"

"How is it again that you and Jordan know each other?"

"Oh, you know, from around." She took a long sip of her wine, whipping her eyes away from Sam seeking any other conversation to hide in. "Carly, I missed what you said about your wife. Where is dear Joanna?"

But before Carly could tell Virginia about her and her wife's latest house fiasco that resulted in Joanna at home with a migraine, Sam reached forward and grabbed Virginia's forearm.

"Gin, where is 'around'?"

"What?" Her attempt to look sincere in her confusion almost brought a smile to her friend's face, but Sam pushed on.

"You said you know Jordan from 'around.' Where is that?"

Virginia laughed, put her wine down, and patted Sam's

hand, who was still grasping Virginia's forearm, reassuringly. "Oh, honey, who can say? I probably met her first through my sister. Maybe it was one of those poetry nights she drags me to, you know, that crowd."

"It was Grasp."

Both women swiveled in their seats, hands still intertwined, to look at Jordan. Sam felt herself flush. Holy matzo, this woman is hot, her inner voice screamed. In all of her immediate confusion and then intense anxiety at running a seder while feeling inexplicably turned on, she hadn't taken the opportunity to really appreciate all of Jordan.

She'd come back in the room with her sleeves rolled up, her floral jacket left on the back of her chair. The top three buttons were undone, a small gold chain with a pomegranate charm laying against her soft skin. Try as she might, Sam failed at not looking down to Jordan's slacks. They were snug around muscular thighs and the well ironed gray material made her think simultaneously of the butch woman's salt and pepper hair and her tight ass that Sam had thought of many times since the day at the store.

As if pulling herself through a sexy molasses, Sam finally processed Jordan's words. Suddenly remembering that Jordan could see her staring at her thighs, she forced herself to look at the other woman's face, where she found an arched brow that set her face on fire.

"So this is typical behavior for you then?" Jordan's mouth pulled into a cocky smirk and she slipped both hands into her pockets, rocking back on her heels. Sam could see Gin's confused look even out of the corner of her eye and she knew she needed to take control of the moment before her friend asked any questions.

"What is 'Grasp?' Sounds like an awful gay men's club." This earned her a snorting laugh from Jordan and a panicked intake of breath from Virginia.

"One-of-those-poetry-nights," Virginia managed all as one word at the same time Jordan was saying, "A dating app."

The world slowed around her and Sam couldn't tell how much of that had to do with the two large glasses of wine the Passover ritual had already provided for her, and how much had to do with the stab of betrayal she was suddenly feeling.

Slowly turning to Virginia, Sam asked, each word its own question, "A? Dating? App?"

Virginia seemed to shrink into her chair for a moment, eyes darting to the other group at the table currently deeply engrossed in a lively debate about the ethics of taxation. Then she seemed to realize there was no escape but the truth and sat up very straight in her chair, turning towards the woman staring daggers into her and fixed her eyes just above Sam's head.

"Well, I told you about that app, the one my sister told me about? The one she said all the lesbians had joined?"

"Yeah, I remember. I also remember telling you to take a hike when you tried to get me to sign up."

"Well, yeah, " Gin glanced over at Jordan who was now leaning against the fridge, arms crossed, a look of oh-boy-I-can't-wait on her face. "But I really just thought if you had a chance to, you know, deal with those," she lowered her voice to a whisper, "cobwebs—"

"Virginia!"

"Fine, fine. I just thought it was about time. Honey, you have so much love to give!" Sam snorted at this, but Gin pushed on, "So, I had Maddy teach me about the app, and I made a little fake profile for you—"

"You did what! What photo did you use?"

"That's what you're worried about?" Gin asked, looking a tiny bit relieved.

"There aren't any photos on the app," Jordan supplied as she finally returned to her seat, her leg bumping Sam's again.

Definitely an accident, Sam thought, even while feeling her thoughts take a turn once again toward what that leg would feel like bare against her own.

The wine, proximity, and absurd situation emboldened her.

What's the worst that can happen? She came expecting a date after all, she thought as she pressed her leg back against Jordan's.

The other woman slid her eyes casually over to read Sam's expression, and whatever she found there seemed to grant her the permission to put a hidden hand upon Sam's bare knee. Fire raced straight up her thigh to—

"Exactly! I barely had to put any identifying information about you on there," Virginia explained, nodding too much as she grasped at the hope that Jordan would be her ally in this effort.

"What?" Sam cleared her throat, her brain clouded with the pressure of the sexy butch's hand on her bare flesh, the gentle stroke of her thumb over the curve of her calf. Something cold made contact with her skin. A thumb ring she hadn't noticed?

"On the app. I basically just had to write what you were looking for, and then a bunch of people responded and I wrote back to them and Jordan was just the clear winner." Virginia trailed off as Sam felt her brows meet in the middle.

"You wrote what I was looking for and then you—" Sam forced herself to make eye contact with Jordan. "Responded? What was it that I was looking for?"

"If I'm remembering correctly, it said something like 'femme Jewish goddess seeks smoking hot butch for a breadless date.'"

"And you thought, oh, I'm in need of a Jewish woman who hates gluten?"

Jordan's laugh was a deep rumble in her chest and Sam's thigh pressed itself farther into the woman's grasp in reflex.

It's definitely the wine, Sam rationed to herself. We're just feeling free. It's the theme of the evening after all.

"I'm also Jewish, Sam. I knew it was a Passover reference. This is the first year that I've only had second night plans. And I figured four glasses of wine is a great way to get to know someone."

"What happened to your first night plans?" Sam asked before finishing the remaining drops of her second glass. She immediately regretted both the drink and the question as she felt Jordan's hand stop stroking and then leave her leg.

"My divorce finalized last summer. We always did the first night with friends and the second night just the two of us. But my friends moved me to their second night list this year, and, uh, well, I won't be seeing Monica for either night. Obviously."

There was a moment of strained silence. Sam's tipsy brain split into several different directions as she scrambled for the right thing to say. Something clever and smooth that would get them back onto whatever track included Jordan's hand on her body.

Gin took in a slow, deep breath before suggesting it was time to move on to the remaining parts of the seder.

"Yes, of course," Sam muttered, pulling her gaze from Jordan's troubled face. She raised her voice to get the whole group's attention. "Ok! We have, oh, only a billion more pages left of this seder before we can actually eat the meal. Carly, why don't you take us into the hand washing and then we'll have some of this gourmet homemade matzo."

"Oh, wait!" Jordan's face lit up and she reached under the table, pulling out her leather backpack. "I forgot I brought a few important things."

She retrieved a baggy of long, bright green scallions,

handed it over to Sam, and then went back in, to then surface with a tupperware of mauve paste.

"What am I looking at here?" Leo asked, stretching toward his wife to get a better view around the geranium centerpieces. Alyssa sweetly put her arm around her husband, kissed his flushed cheek and pushed back against him to balance his chair. Sam felt the tightening in her chest. She loved her friends so much.

"Oh man, are you Persian?" Carly asked, taking the tupperware out of Jordan's hands. "Is this charoset?"

"Haleq, Persian charoset, yes." Then, turning to Sam, she added, "I hope you don't mind, it's just not Passover unless I have some of my mom's haleq."

"No, I love that you brought it." Sam almost winced at the amount of warmth she heard in her own voice. "I'm excited to try it. Where is your mom, your family?"

"Back in Baltimore. I call her every year and have her tell me what to do. This year she held out on me until I promised to come home next year for Nowruz and Passover. I'm the only one of my siblings who moved so far away."

Sam loved the way the skin around Jordan's eyes softened and crinkled while she talked about her mom. She imagined her own eyes must have turned into cartoon hearts after all of her tender gazing.

"And those scallions are for hitting each other?" Alyssa asked, interrupting Sam's swooning.

"Excuse me?" Virginia asked, taking the bag of onions from Sam.

"When we sing Dayenu, Persian families smack each other with spring onions. I think some people use scallions, and it was also all that the store had. I thought I could bring that custom with me too."

And so the night proceeded with increasingly drunken storytelling and singing. They all energetically hit each other with scallions and danced around the table. Alyssa stood upon a chair and recited a poem she'd memorized as a child but replaced all the adjectives with dirty words. Carly, much to Sam's embarrassment and everyone else's delight, found a picture of a Passover from years earlier where Sam had fallen asleep in her bright green armchair with a Moses beard on.

When they ran out of traditional songs to sing, from everyone's own version of Judaism, they started in on secular songs that felt thematic. Sam tried to keep calm when Jordan pulled her close and shimmied them around the table to the tune of "500 Miles" by The Proclaimers. She utterly failed and saw all of her friends look at her with soft, hopeful expressions that caused her stomach to flip.

* * *

When everyone was done eating, and the afikomen was forgotten, and the wine bottles had been drained and gathered into the recycling bin, Sam said a teary, grateful goodbye to Alyssa, Leo, and Carly as they headed out for their rideshare.

She turned back to Virginia and Jordan, both of whom were packing up their bags, and thanked them for the tenth time, "Thank you both so much. I don't know what I would have done without you, either of you. And that matzo was so much better than the boxed kind, wasn't it?"

"It was still a tasteless cracker, but yes, better," Virginia teased as she closed her purse. "As the only sober person at this shindig I was less seduced by the matzo, but still proud of us for making it. I've got to get home though, who knows when my patient will go into labor. Jordan, do you need a ride home?"

"I was planning to stay and help clean up. We got a little wild there at the end." Jordan sent another wink in Sam's direction.

"Oh, you don't need to do-" Sam started before Virginia shot her a mischievous look and spoke over her.

"Ok, great, so nice to meet, I mean, see you, Jordan." Virginia said, scurrying to the front door, only stopping to place a quick kiss on Sam's cheek. And adding, as she left the front door, "Great job, honey. Don't stay up too late."

And then there were just the two of them. Sam's eyes went wide with the realization. She went to the door, locked it behind Virginia and paused for a moment before turning around and putting her back against it.

Jordan was suddenly a lot closer than she'd been a moment earlier. Later, when she told this story, the story of their first kiss, she'd focus on other details, but in the moment her mind kept returning to the temperature of the other woman's body. She could feel the heat rippling off of her from inches away. It was so seductive, like the flames of desire themselves. She wanted to cocoon herself in Jordan's heat, to let this walking flame thaw the frozen walls she feared were permanently around her heart.

The taller woman reached out, placing a hand on either side of Sam's head against the door and leaning in close. "I guess we should get cleaning, hm?"

"Um, yeah, sure, that sounds great." Sam's voice came out husky and low, suggesting anything but tidying. She licked her lips, finding the heat between them to be almost too much, and watched Jordan's eyes trace the same path across her mouth. And that was it, they came together instantly, Sam reaching up to thread her fingers through Jordan's hair, Jordan bunching the sides of Sam's dress in her fists, exposing inches more of previously hidden thigh.

Their mouths were hard and soft in turns, giving and taking in equal measure. Sam caught Jordan's lower lip between her teeth and tugged, the other woman making a sound dangerously close to a whimper.

She pressed herself to as much of Jordan as she could, her left thigh coming up to caress the outside of Jordan's leg and even just that, just the heat radiating off of the still clothed butch into Sam's exposed skin brought a rumbling moan from her throat.

They stood in her entryway making out and moving their hands across expanses of fabric and skin for seconds, days, hours. The wine and arousal stripping time of all meaning. Until Sam's cell phone buzzed insistently and both of them seemed to remember themselves.

"Do you need to get that?" Jordan asked, her eyes dark with need.

"It's probably just Gin telling me she got home in one piece." Sam moved into Jordan once more, before her phone buzzed a second, third, and fourth time. She sighed, letting her head gently thump against the door behind her as she fished the phone from her dress pocket.

There were a series of texts from Virginia that began with "OMG, HOT HOT HOT" and ranged to "Oh I'm home btw" and "I need EVERY DETAIL TOMORROW, I am a world champion MATCHMAKER AND I DESERVE A PRIZE." Sam shook her head at the phone but couldn't help the goofy smile that crept across her lips. She ran a hand over her face to help contain it.

"Did she get home ok?" Jordan asked from inches away, her pelvis still pressing into Sam's, her fingers clutching at Sam's ass.

"Yes, and is otherwise the nosiest person alive," she let out a giggle. "Sorry to have interrupted this-" she swept a hand between the two of them, indicating the wildly hot makeout that had occurred moments before. "We can return to the regularly scheduled programming now."

Jordan leaned forward, gently rubbing her soft lips against Sam's. The shorter woman gasped and opened her mouth a tiny bit to let in more air. The kiss was different from their frantic energy moments earlier. Jordan took her time exploring Sam's mouth, sliding her tongue teasingly along the inner ridge of each lip and then flicking it against the other woman's tongue. Sam let her explore, scrunching the butch woman's shirt up out of her slacks and crawling her fingers under the fabric to tickle and tease the skin beneath.

After a particularly deep kiss, Jordan leaned back and said, "Why don't we get those leftovers put away and then we can move this to the bedroom?"

Sam felt her mouth go suddenly dry with nervous antici-pation and just nodded, not trusting her voice to come out at an audible decibel.

They threw the food quickly into some tupperware, and then Jordan insisted on setting some of the plates in the sink to soak. Sam stacked the decorations into keep and recycle piles, sneaking glances at Jordan at her sink every few seconds. There was something unfairly hot about how she stood, feet knee distance apart, shirt wrinkled and free of her slacks, a kitchen towel thrown over her shoulder, sleeves rolled up to her elbows.

Jordan looked back over her shoulder to catch Sam's eye and throw her another wink. She felt herself melting in response. "I also brought some whisky in my bag."

"What?" Sam blinked at her, realizing she had been lost in Jordan's eyes and hadn't heard a word she said.

"If you want to share a nightcap, I brought some whisky."

Sam cleared her throat and nodded, turning to pull down a beautiful pink crystal glass she'd found at a thrift shop and then reached blindly into Jordan's backpack to find the bottle. Her hand closed around something distinctly not a glass bottle and she froze. Just at that moment, Jordan turned off the water, pulled the towel off her shoulder to dry her hands and turned around, catching sight of Sam's expression.

"Oh. Yeah, should have said I brought a few other things too." Jordan laughed and moved forward to find the whisky herself.

"Is my hand around your cock right now?" Sam asked in a low voice.

"One of them, yes."

"You brought a dildo to a stranger's house?" Again, the incredible confidence of this woman! Sam felt more shocked by that than anything else.

"And a few other tools," Jordan admitted with a mischievous smirk.

"Why!" It came out more exclamation than question.

"I was a Girl Scout, always prepared, etcetera." Jordan reached forward and wrapped her fingers around Sam's wrist, pulling her hand out of her bag. Sam remembered at the last moment to let go of the silicone dick and it thumped back down into the bag.

Sam backed up a step or two, giving Jordan some space as she fished out the bottle of whisky, uncorked it and poured some into the glass Sam still held. We're going to have sex, Sam realized. Like, sex-sex with maybe her dick inside of me, sex. Her whole body trembled and she took a big swig of the liquor to still her thoughts. It didn't work.

Jordan took the glass from her and took her own sip, maintaining eye contact with Sam. Sam felt a mist of sweat along her upper lip and wondered if there were sweat marks under her arms. What is wrong with me? Sam wondered as Jordan put the glass down on the table and stepped closer, a hand coming out to rest on Sam's waist. Sam was certain that Jordan could feel her sudden full body sweat and would likely be disturbed by the surprising additional lubrication. Before Jordan could pull her closer she stepped away again and squeaked out, "Actually, I don't think I can do this."

Jordan stood perfectly still, a hand still out in the air between them where Sam's waist had previously been.

Sam thought she was probably hoping holding it out like that would dry it off. *Disgusting*, she groaned to herself.

After a few seconds passed, Sam wondered if Jordan had heard her and cleared her voice to say it again.

"Ok, that's fine. I'll call a car," Jordan said and moved the hand to grab her bag instead. Her tone was casual, as if they were merely rescheduling brunch plans and not going from a hundred miles an hour to a deadstop. "Thanks again for having me, and for teaching me how to make matzo."

"Yes, of course, yeah, thank you, I mean, for making it," Sam stammered out, torn between wanting the other woman's hands on her again and wanting her to already be gone.

"I'll wait for my ride outside." Jordan smiled a stranger's smile at Sam and pulled her backpack on as she headed to the front door.

"You don't have to do that, you could-"

"No, it's fine, it'll give me a chance to," she hesitated for a second as she pulled the door open, turned and shot Sam a warm smile, "cool off. Have a good night, Sam."

And then she was gone, the door shut behind her, and Sam was left to press the heels of her hands to her eyes and groan loudly enough to fill her empty, still apartment.

Chapter Six

"Gin, my head," Sam groaned in response to her best friend's squeal of delight when she answered the phone. Sam clutched at her temples as she tried again to push against gravity and make it out of the bed.

"I offered you my grape juice, honey, this is a monster of your own creation," came Virginia's overly peppy voice through the cell's speaker.

"Right now is really not the time for I-told-you-so's." Again Sam gave up on getting free of the comforter and slumped back into the sheets. She'd woken up an hour earlier, drained the large glass of water on the bedside table—*thank you, drunk Sam*—and then stared blurrily at the ceiling for fifty minutes until her phone started vibrating with Virginia's call.

"Fine, but it is the time for tell-me-what-happened's."

Sam merely groaned again in response and rolled over to bury her face in the pillow.

"I don't know how to read that, Sam. Was that a, 'I just had the best sex of my life, thank you for putting together a set-up you wonderful creature' or a 'I hate you forever, Jordan robbed me while I was in the bathroom and this is why you don't bring strangers over' groan?"

"So, you thought it was possible that she might be a burglar and you still left me alone with her?" Sam asked after rolling back onto her back and cursing the day wine was invented.

"No, I mean, it would be very surprising if she'd turned out to be anything other than perfect given the googling I did of her before I brought her to yours, but anything's possible, I suppose."

"She was a perfect gentleman."

"And yet you sound miserable."

"We made out from the minute you left until you texted me you were home. Like tipsy teenagers."

"Well, that is promising!" Virginia's voice hit an octave that seemed to shake loose yet another level of hangover from Sam and she held the phone farther from her head.

"Sure, until I utterly panicked and basically threw her out."

"What!"

"Gin, for real, my head. I am almost thirty-one years old, clearly no longer capable of holding my drink, and I cannot have you screaming at me."

"I'm sorry, Sam," she whispered. "Why did you throw her out?"

"I told you, I panicked," Sam practically whined into the phone. She scowled as she remembered the frozen look on Jordan's face and her own inability to explain herself.

"Well, yes, I heard that." Virginia's voice was uncharacteristically patient. "But what did you panic about? You don't think you have actual cobwebs, right? Because, honey, that's just a figure-"

"Gin, please, stop talking about my vagina." Sam sighed noisily and pushed herself up to a sitting position. "I don't know why I freaked out. I think it was just so fast. I mean, she's a total stranger."

"Not a *total*-"

"Virginia Emily, she is a stranger you met on the internet. There are dozens of podcasts about the dangers of that."

"Fine, but this is still great! You felt something, you made out! Was the kissing good?" Virginia's southern drawl stretched the o's in good out until the word sounded positively filthy.

"So good." Sam sighed. "Like toe curling good."

Her best friend's response was an ear-splitting squeal.

"But that doesn't matter," Sam continued soberly, "I mean, the chemistry was out of control, but maybe that was just the wine. And I basically shoved her out the door at the end of the night, so that's it, just a fun makeout."

"No! You can definitely fix this, you just need to call her. I can give you her number."

"I don't know, Gin. I think I'm going to let this one go, I don't want to force anything. Let's talk about something else, anything other than my dating life. How's your patient? Any news?"

"Ok, ok, but I'll say love doesn't just happen, you have to help it along." She took a deep breath that Sam worried would turn into a lecture, but instead Gin blew out a raspberry and said, "This woman just will not give birth. We're connecting in twenty minutes to discuss inducing her."

"Fun." Sam winced. "Well, I hope it all goes smoothly."

"You and me both," Virginia said. "So, what are you and your hangover up to today?"

"Remind myself I'm an adult," Sam murmured. She cleared her throat and continued at an audible level, "Bring some good, new energy into this place. I think I'll do a whole spring clean, air it all out. And I have Cara and T's seder tonight. I *need* to go buy some grape juice, I can't even think about wine right now."

* * *

And so, Sam broke out her all-natural cleaning supplies and took out her sexual frustration on the counters, floor, and backsplash in the kitchen. She ran a load of laundry in the building's one shared washer-dryer set and chowed down on seder leftovers between chores.

When she went to put away her neatly rolled and folded earl gray bath towels she found a surprise. Gently placed atop her only remaining clean towel was her favorite kitchen dish towel with the drawings of pigeons as chefs. It was folded neatly into a square and as she picked it up, a piece of matzo fell out, along with a folded piece of paper. The afikomen, she thought, we totally forgot to search for it.

She tossed the flat bread into the bathroom trash to be taken out when she was done with her thorough clean. And then she picked up the paper. It was a small sheet of stationary Jordan must have brought from home. Really, her backpack had been like Mary Poppins. It was creamy white with a thin dark green border and what Sam assumed were her initials— JM—embossed in the corner.

All that was sprawled across it in tiny, neat handwriting was "S, I want you, J" and what she assumed was the stranger's phone number. She read the words several times, each time sending a jolt shooting straight down her legs before her brain caught up and thought—what the fuck? What if someone else had found this? What if they'd all remembered to look for the afikomen?

But that only makes it hotter, some horny voice inside her whispered. That was so much of the appeal of Jordan. Well, aside from her looks, her toned butt, her fathomless eyes, her

—Sam shook her head as if to dislodge the intrusive sexy thoughts. She crumpled up the paper, tossed it in with the discarded matzo, and returned to her chores.

* * *

After finding the note, every few minutes she'd catch herself remembering the feel of Jordan's hands on her waist, the soft resistance of her lips against her own, and she'd flush, attempt to redirect her thoughts to the tasks at hand, and then start the cycle all over again.

Eventually she made her way into the bedroom to rip the sheets off and give her room the same fresh start as the rest of the apartment. But then her eye caught the ancient felt box under the bedside table filled with her favorite toys and that, coupled with the constant intrusion of the memory of how well Jordan wore pants, was too much for her self-control.

She flopped back onto the bed, reaching behind and below her to fish out her favorite vibrator, and allowed the memories of the night before to flood her senses. Jordan's scent, wood, campfire, sugar, surrounded her as she shimmied her hips out of her sweatpants. She remembered the feel of Jordan's thick, cold thumb ring sliding against the exposed flesh of her thigh under the Passover table. She imagined that instead of putting her foot in her mouth about Jordan's private life, she had leaned closely, fluttered her lashes at the butch woman, said something low and seductive that would cause Jordan's hand to tighten on her leg. She'd slide her body closer, inch by inch, encouraging the stranger to slide her palm higher up her leg below the skirt of Sam's dress.

She turned the vibrator on and began to trace it up the same path she imagined Jordan's fingers would have followed. Her breath grew shallower and she felt her lower back arch a bit off the mattress. Some small voice in the back of her mind was laughing, she hadn't had a crush, especially one as hopeless as this, in so many years. But she shut that voice out by falling back into her imagination.

There had been something so delicious about Jordan's hand on her knee just out of sight of her friends. Sam had never thought herself one for exhibitionism before, but she couldn't deny that it had been a significant part of what was making her wet now. Jordan had been so brave, or reckless, Sam couldn't decide which. They had been strangers, they still were strangers. She wanted to drink in that confidence, feel what it must be like to go after what you want with abandon.

As she trailed the vibrator higher, she imagined Jordan's hand had traced all the way to the soaking center of her thighs, that her fingertips had met with the silk underwear she'd had on during the seder and had begun to trace small, enticing circles on the fabric. Lulling Sam into a sense of safety, even though anyone could have noticed how close their bodies had moved, the motion of Jordan's arm, mostly hidden below the tablecloth.

Sam would have taken a page out of Jordan's book and gone for what she wanted, sliding her legs apart, careful to angle herself toward Jordan and not accidentally tip Virginia off to what was happening just beside her. Jordan's fingers would have hooked around the side of Sam's underwear, tugging them down just enough to slip into them, slowly opening her, continuing to circle her fingertips against the skin until she found the spot she'd been seeking.

In her bed, Sam gasped as her vibrator finally made contact with her clit. Her whole body was electrified with unmet need. She knew she'd only last a moment. She thought of Jordan again, this time standing at the end of the bed, fully dressed in her dark jeans and pressed button-up, arms crossed, leaning against the dresser with a smirk on her face. She imagined her party guests were still just on the other side of the door, clueless to what the two women were doing in her bedroom. She gasped as she rode a crest closer to coming, and in her mind Jordan lifted one finger to her own smiling lips, reminding her to be quiet and not alert her friends. The stranger pushed away from the dresser, stalking toward the bed and Sam, whispering the words she'd written in her note, *I want you.*

And Sam was gone, lost to her imaginings, to the swell of need and lust and hope.

Chapter Seven

As Sam walked up the long, winding garden path from the street to Cara and T's new place, she noticed all the ways the couple had melded their identities together in the decor. Cara was into wrought iron and driftwood, T nearly always wore floral patterns and lace. The garden featured a bench and chair set in Cara's typical style that had been painted with delicate abstract flowers and lavender had been planted wildly amongst long native grasses.

Cara and T had moved in together after several years of casually dating. Sam had always admired their relationship, but in a way of distance and difference. Cara and T were both polyamorous, had been what they would have called "casual play partners," introduced during a threesome with a partner they had in common.

Sam wasn't sure what had ever become of that third person, she was pretty sure the woman had been married and in an open relationship with her husband, but that was the extent of her knowledge. What she did know was what she'd been able to observe over the last few years. Cara and T had stayed in each other's orbits and pulled closer and closer over time until one day Cara and Sam went out to brunch and Cara had burst into tears. "I'm madly in love with them," she'd wept into her mimosa.

Sam had laughed and gently rubbed a hand along Cara's back, reminding her that this was a wonderful, beautiful thing. Cara had been so worried that T would find her old fashioned if she expressed her desires to them and that had sent Sam into another fit of laughter. Nothing about her friend was "old-fashioned."

Shortly after that morning, Cara had called to announce that she'd talked to T, that they felt the same way, and that they were going to move in together.

Sam had whooped and cheered over the phone and felt her heart glow for her friend's happiness. She knew she wasn't interested in polyamory herself, but she envied the honesty and intention with which Cara and T entered into their life together.

Now she was twenty minutes late because of the alone time she'd spent thinking about a hot butch she'd likely never see again. She blushed as she knocked on their bright blue door, wondering if she had "Just Masturbated" written all over her reddening cheeks.

T pulled the door open, laughing at something happening inside and then immediately pulled Sam simultaneously into a firm hug and in out of the cold, smoothly shutting the door behind Sam's back. They smelled like chicken soup and the earth. "Hey pal! We were worried you were still so hungover from yesterday you were going to miss tonight."

"Why would you assume I'm hungover? I'm a grown ass woman, I can handle four glasses of wine." She said as she unwrapped her arms from T's neck.

"Sure, but then also the whisky-" T trailed off, eyes going wide.

"How do you know about the whisky?" Sam asked, squinting her eyes in suspicion.

"Oops! I should probably lie and say I just assumed. I know you hosted last night and it was Saturday and you love whisky. *So*—" They dragged out the vowel, clearly looking for a way out of their misstep. "It just makes sense that you'd get schnockered? But—" They trailed off again for a second, glancing back over their shoulder. "Well, seems you and I have a new mutual friend. New for you, old—very old—for me. And she may have clued us in on your liberating festivities."

Sam felt her eyebrows meet in confusion before T moved out of the way and she spotted Jordan seated comfortably at one of the two set tables visible in the main room. The butch woman was leaning the chair back on two legs, one ankle on the opposite knee, hands clasped behind her head. Jordan was dressed in a soft rust colored button up with a dotted pattern in a slighter darker shade, dark gray slacks, and leather sneakers. It all brought out the gold in her tan complexion and the warmth in her brown eyes. Commanding, at ease, smoking hot. Immediately her cheeks flushed to a vibrant pink, and a stirring in her stomach thrummed for her attention as she tried to ignore the rushing sensation she felt at the sight. "Jordan."

"Exactly!" T laughed, clapping Sam on the back. "What a small, gay world. Anyway, we haven't even started yet. Cara has been telling everyone the traumatic U-haul story of getting all of her shit into this house. We've all been interrupting to make U-haul jokes. I think everyone will be relieved to get to that first glass of wine."

They walked Sam to her seat, luckily, or unluckily, at the table where Jordan was not. As she settled into one of the four mismatched chairs, she realized she and Jordan were seated facing each other at opposite corners. She busied herself rummaging through her purse to pull out the grape juice she'd brought to use instead of wine. Her head still felt a little tight at the temples.

She didn't hear T talking until they asked, "Sam? Did you hear me?"

"What? No, sorry. You're right, after all. I am still a bit hungover."

T smiled understandingly and asked, again, "How do you know Jordan? Once she found out you were the Samantha we were waiting on she was eager to share how much wine the two of you had made it through last night. But then she was annoyingly tight-lipped about how she ended up at your place." T shot a childish look at Jordan, who was engrossed in a conversation with Josh and Cara, but returned the look. Sam almost snorted in surprise. "I'd assume mutual friends, but I think I know every single one of Jordan's friends."

"Uh, well, it was a set-up. You know Virginia?" T nodded. "Well, she's doing her best to get me off the market as quickly as possible."

Cara had left her conversation with Josh and Jordan to walk up behind T and greet Sam. Cara snaked her arms around T's middle, leaning her head on their shoulder and waggling her eyebrows at Sam. "I hate that phrase, Sam. 'The market.' Ugh, disgusting. But I think you and Jordan sound hot, hot, hot together."

Sam's eyebrows shot up and she chanced a wide-eyed glance at Jordan, who seemed to not have heard from across the two tables. "Stop! There's nothing there. She's recently divorced, I'm still recovering. Ships in the night and all that."

T's face contorted at the mention of Jordan's divorce, but before Sam could ask about it, Cara was pushing them into the seat to Sam's left and announcing to the group that the tardy party had arrived and they could begin. Sam flushed again remembering why she'd been late.

"Let's start with introductions. I think we should do it like this: I'll introduce the person to my right, say how I know them, ask their pronouns, and then they'll introduce the person to their right, on and on." She took her seat at Jordan's table, her legs folded underneath her in the maroon armchair she'd pulled up to the well-appointed card table. "To my right, sort of, is my love, T."

Everyone spontaneously awed and then dissolved into surprised collective laughter. "T and I met in my bed." She paused to raise an eyebrow suggestively and look daringly around the room. No one was scandalized and she rolled her eyes. "What pronouns do you use, darling?"

"They, them." T, who was seated at the next table, but almost within Cara's arm's reach, grinned like a fool at their lover before making eye contact with Sam. "This is Sam. Sam and I met through Cara, and the first thing Sam said to me was 'I love getting new best-friends-in-laws.' Pronouns, dude?"

"Well, I do love new best friends I don't even have to make! I use she/her. To my right is Lanie. Hi, Lanie. Oh, and sorry I was late, everyone. Lanie and I have known each other since college, strangely enough. We both went to a weird arts school in Indiana and met at the gay students' club. There were only three of us, which was even weirder. I mean, *art,* you all, *art.* Lanie, pronouns?"

"She, her. That was the weirdest college. I only stayed a year, but Sam's a trooper and made it all the way through. Ok, this is Evelyn." She reached out and grasped Evelyn's forearm. "Our resident straight person. Unless there's news?"

Evelyn laughed and shook her head. "No, sorry, still a hetero. But I can't be the only one. Josh, are you straight?" She twisted in her seat to see Josh at the other table behind her.

"No, love, sorry. Big ol' bisexual."

"Oh, fine." Evelyn pretended to pout for a second before laughing.

"So, our straighty," Lanie continued. "Evelyn and I met in

a Black women's financial empowerment seminar like twelve years ago. She was the one who kept raising her hand and asking things like, 'but shouldn't we be tearing down the system?' and I knew we had to be best friends."

"Lane, you're supposed to ask me my pronouns, too! Don't worry, I got you: she/her. To my right, well, behind me really, is Megan." She turned all the way round in her chair to look at Megan at the other table, who was fighting with the tablecloth in order to also turn and make eye contact with Evelyn.

"Megan and I met at last year's seder when I tried to steal Megan's coat. Pronouns?"

"Not if I can help it," Megan replied. "And yeah, this bitch walked right off with my peacoat, which was mauve, a thousand shades away from her lavender jacket."

A brief argument broke out about the sheer ridiculousness of that claim, and what was mauve anyway? And Josh was certain it was actually green until Cara started chanting chartreuse and T had to beg everyone to get on with the introductions.

"Ok, I'm just going to speed this along because otherwise we'll never get out of here," Cara melodramatically moaned to the group as she stood and waved her haggadah at everyone. "Megan and Jordan just met like an hour ago when Megan almost smacked Jordan in the face with the fridge door. Jordan, pronouns?"

"She, her."

"Great, this is Josh, we met in the same gender processing, trans therapy, weepy feely group where we met Megan, I don't know if Josh knows Jordan but now everyone knows everyone and the show can begin!" Cara plopped back into her seat and fanned herself with the haggadah.

"I use he, him," Josh offered to the room and Cara laughed about forgetting her own rules. This set the group off on yet another explosion of comments about rules and the spirit of the holiday and everyone who'd just learned several new names immediately forgot them. Sam found that even sober she was having difficulty following the high speed banter around her.

Everyone avoided using names or pronouns at all costs, which only added to the confusion and also seemed to bring Megan a considerable amount of joy.

* * *

An hour and a half later, they all took a break to stretch their legs, hydrate, and go on a quest to find the afikomen T had hidden an hour earlier. Sam halfheartedly poked around the living room, sneaking long looks from the corner of her eye to watch Jordan as the woman joked around with Cara about something that seemed to require a lot of pantomiming what might have been a saxophone.

"Why are you being such a creep?" Lanie asked close to Sam's ear.

Sam felt herself literally jump before she whipped around to face her old friend. "Lanie! Why! Why do you think I deserve a heart attack!"

"I just asked you a question, creep." Lanie laughed. "You're the one over here staring at Cara like you're afraid she's going to disappear."

"I'm not staring at Cara," Sam said before she realized her mistake. "I mean—"

"Oh?" Lanie raised an eyebrow. "You're not? You're badly spying on this hot masc snack? What was their name again?"

"Her name is Jordan," Sam muttered, feeling her face flush.

"Oh, so you're remembering names and everything. I

don't feel like I even know your name anymore after the chaos of this evening."

"We...well, she was at my seder last night, too." Sam looked just over Lanie's head to avoid revealing anything else with her guilty, sex-crazed eyes.

"What! Why? How do you know each other?" Lanie crossed her arms and narrowed her eyes. "And why are you acting so weird?"

"Uh, I'm not, I'm just hungover," Sam lied unconvincingly.

"Mhm, you know, I'm going to call you for all the details this weekend, so don't think you're getting out of that, missy, but right now your lover boy just walked into the hallway and you obviously have something you need to say to her." Lanie made a shooing motion with her hand while she smiled angelically at Sam.

Sam groaned, but did as she was told and followed Jordan into the hallway, where the taller woman was making a mockery of searching by rubbing down the walls and feeling around the door jambs.

"What are you doing?" Sam asked, causing Jordan to look over her shoulder at her while she rubbed a finger along the top of one door.

"Well, hello to you too."

"I waved when I came in," Sam murmured in embarrassment.

"Did you? It looked like T told you I was here and then you went white as a sheet. I don't remember any waving." Jordan took her hands off of the wall and shoved them in her pockets.

"I'm just white, that's sort of how I always look, and I thought about waving. Does that count?" Before Jordan could answer, Sam reached out and pulled open the door in front of them to reveal a coat closet. "We should at least try to actually look."

They both stood in silence, staring at one another for a moment. But the hallway was tight, so when Josh entered the hallway as well and needed to open the bathroom door, he placed a hand on Jordan's back and announced, "sorry, just going to put you back into the closet for a second so I can squeeze past!"

Josh laughed at his own closet joke, and Jordan stepped into the closet with Sam. The door shut behind them, leaving them in almost complete darkness. Sam heard the song on T's playlist switch to Robyn and Cara's whooping before the song was turned up loud enough that the base vibrated in the walls.

They both waited in total stillness to give Josh enough time to open and close the bathroom door and then Sam heard Jordan's hand hit the metal of the knob in the quieter interior of the closet. Then, a low curse came from too close to Sam's ear.

"The inner knob doesn't turn."

At once, they both began to feel around for a light switch. As she silently cursed her terrible luck, Sam felt something gently land on her nose and shrieked. When she reached up to pull it off her face, it turned out to be the light switch, they were suddenly bathed in soft red light.

"Of course T would put a mood light in a closet," Jordan said as she rolled her eyes.

"I mean, haven't you been to the bathroom yet? It's like a bathhouse in there."

"That's the least surprising thing I've heard tonight." They both laughed, Sam realized she was close to giggling and the blush that would not dissipate flamed on.

"At least we can hear in here, I never realized Cara was such a Robyn fan."

"I mean, who isn't a Robyn fan?" And then they both

stood quietly for a moment, taking in the lack of space between and around their bodies,

"So, you've known T a while, huh?" Just a normal, casual conversation between two people locked in tremendously close proximity, Sam thought as she pushed her back against the wall.

"Yeah, I gave them their first job." Jordan shoved her hands into her pockets as she spoke. "Well, *job* is maybe going a bit far. I let them fuck around at my shop and they got paid in wood."

"They got paid in dick? Like dildos?" Sam almost whispered the question in her disbelief.

"What! What the hell are you talking about?"

"You said you paid them in 'wood.'"

Jordan gaped at Sam for a second longer before she began to laugh. The butch woman put her hands on her thighs and leaned forward a bit while she took a few deep breaths. This put her short cropped salt and pepper hair within sniffing distance of Sam's face. She caught sandalwood and smoke before turning her face away and crossing her arms.

"I wasn't trying to be funny."

"Oh, I know." Jordan reached up and grasped Sam's biceps, using her grip to straighten up, but her hands lingered there. "That makes it even funnier. That was so goofy."

"I'm not goofy!"

"Not at all, but what? Paid in wood led you to dildos? Where's your mind at?"

"Hmmph," was all Sam managed as she fought the urge to lean toward the woman still holding her.

"That's the kind of impression I've given you? That I'd say something that ridiculous?"

"No! I mean, I don't know. I don't know why that's what popped into my head." Except she did know why, and her face reddened once more with the memory of how she'd spent her afternoon. "I mean, you do carry a dildo around in your backpack!"

"Fair enough. But, no, they were a scrawny, pimply teenager. I thought of them as an awkward kid who'd wandered into my shop. And they knew my youngest sister from summer camp or elementary school or something, so I was trying to do her a favor as well."

"Your shop? Like you own a home goods store?"

"Why do you assume home goods?"

"Well, again, the wood." And the smell of her, the rich, velvety smoke scent. Plus she dressed elegantly, like the butch version of a renovation tv show host.

"Ah, I see. Sort of. I'm a carpenter and a woodworker. Now I mostly make custom shelving, the whole open shelves look has made for good business these last few years." She finally released her hold and Sam felt the absence of those strong hands straight to her core.

Damn it, she wasn't even drinking this time, but every moment with this woman felt intoxicating. Her low voice, her sexy ass clothing, and now this butch as hell job.

Sam nodded her understanding and they both fell again into a tense quiet for a moment. Each of them searching the other's face for a hint of shared feeling.

"I found your note," Sam finally said.

"I was wondering when you would. You didn't text me, so I assumed I'd either hidden it too well, or whatever happened last night was still true today." Jordan's eyes were focused on Sam's mouth, but her brows were drawn together in confusion and concern.

"Part of what happened last night is still true," Sam whispered, her own eyes sweeping across Jordan's features, all softened in this red light. She felt her heart throw itself mercilessly against her ribs, deciding not to mention the note was now in her trash can.

"Which part is still true?" Jordan's voice was almost inaudible, the confident veneer slipping away for a moment to reveal the chasm of vulnerability underneath.

"The part where I wanted you too."

In the moment where chest met chest, hands gripping whatever was closest, and both moved toward falling under the spell they started weaving the night before, the door was suddenly opened. They fell away from each other just as quickly, Jordan literally falling, her body disappearing into the coats.

"Here you are! I thought you'd both left without saying anything until I saw Jordan's backpack. This closet door is terrible, didn't mean to trap y'all." T stood in the doorway, hands on their hips and a knowing glint in their eye. "Jordan, why don't you be a pal and fix this damn door sometime?"

Jordan resurfaced from the hanging tweeds and velvets, clutching T's hand for support and in the other hand grasping the silk scarf wrapped afikomen. "I found it."

"Hooray!" T turned and added over their shoulder, "Jordan found the matzo!" They pulled Jordan's body the rest of the way free of the closet, clasped them in a quick hug and said, "That doesn't get you out of fixing this door though. And Sam, where is your matzo toffee thing?"

"Oh shit!" Sam swore as she stepped blinking into the brighter lights of the house. "I totally forgot it."

Everyone in the kitchen groaned in disappointment, except for Jordan who turned, her arm still around T, and shot Sam a wink.

"Oh shit," Sam said again, but this time just to herself.

* * *

The night was coming to a close, some of the guests making their exit when Sam checked her phone and saw three missed texts from Virginia. This first was an all caps celebration, "BABY CONOVER IS HERE AND CUTE AS A BUTTON! FASTEST LABOR OF MY CAREER." The second was a picture of a very angry, tiny infant swaddled in a beautiful multicolored woven blanket. And the final text had come almost an hour later, "I'm pooped—party bfast w the girls tomorrow?"

Sam shot back a quick 'yes, yes, yes,' before scanning the room for Jordan.

They made eye contact and silently motioned to one another their mutual desire to leave together. They each said their goodbyes, shared their gratitude, and agreed to everything asked of them so they could exit quickly. Cara looked between the two of them with a raised eyebrow, but asked nothing as T drunkenly called to her from somewhere else in the house.

As soon as the front door closed behind them, Jordan reached out and grabbed Sam's hand, pulling her close and wordlessly marching them both to the street-parked faded blue pick-up truck.

"You drive a truck."

"Is that a question?" Jordan laughed, opening the passenger door for Sam.

"No, just making sure this is real life," Sam replied, a goofy smile on her face as she slid onto the truck's dark leather seat.

"Are you saying I'm too good to be true?" Jordan asked moments later when she'd pulled herself into the driver's seat.

"Something like that," Sam admitted, suddenly very preoccupied with untwisting her seatbelt. After a few moments she looked up and realized they were headed in the direction of her apartment. "Do you live near me?"

"Not at all, I live in the opposite direction actually. But I thought I might as well give you a ride home. I know you don't own a car after that rant you went on last night about the evils of fossil fuels." Jordan took her eyes off the road for a second to wink over at Sam. "So, I'm sure this truck's really not doing it for you."

"I mean, you carpooled with Gin last night, that's something."

"Sure, but I was drinking. I'm not going to claim to be a friend to the trees, though I'd like to get better about it."

"You're like the opposite of a friend to the trees, you're a tree butcher," Sam teased.

"I'll have to change my business cards, right now it just says 'woodworker,' but maybe I'll break into the supervillain world if I add 'tree murderer.' I hear the villain community has a real need for oversized desks, might be a smart move for me."

"Wow, I had no idea you were such a nerd." Sam laughed and reached out to put a brave hand on Jordan's thigh.

"Pssh, I'm too old to be a nerd," Jordan said, moving one hand from the steering wheel to wrap around the one Sam had placed in her lap.

"I don't think that's the way it works."

When they reached Sam's building, Jordan pulled over and put the truck in park, cutting the engine. "I'm not expecting anything, just don't want you yelling at me for an idling engine."

"Yelling! Do I seem like the kind of person to yell?" Sam asked, fake indignation pulling her eyebrows up.

"Fine, you caught me. I really just don't want to disappoint you. I'm trying to *impress* you, you know." There was something raw and edgy in the look Jordan gave her and she felt the rise of panic she'd experienced last night just before ending things.

"Well then, you better kiss me."

Jordan's mouth was soft and sweet, her tongue a gentle pressure inside Sam's mouth, distracting her so that she barely noticed the hand that slipped beneath the hem of her dress until fingers lightly caressed the front of her lace underwear. She jumped as they traced a circle against her.

"Are you sensitive there, Sam?" Fingertips followed a lazy pattern against the lace, up, back, around, over and over, causing Sam to gasp into Jordan's mouth.

She welcomed it when Jordan deepened the kiss, as confident and commanding as always, and she spread her legs when the fingers sought out the edges of her panties, pulling them aside. She was close to whimpering as the strokes neared her core, when the image of the note with Jordan's phone number —*I want you*—popped into her head. She stilled and rested a hand on Jordan's arm.

"What's wrong?" Jordan's voice was hoarse, as if she'd just been weeping, or screaming with pleasure.

"I just want to check-in," Sam said, and then looked around them at the street she lived on. "And also, maybe we should take this inside."

"Ok, yeah, sure," Jordan said, nodding and extracting herself from their makeout. "What do you want to check in about?"

"Well, if we'd gone on a real date, instead of being set up, I would have told you I'm recently single, and this is my first time doing...anything since then." Sam paused to take in a deep breath, steadying her wavering voice. "And I'm curious what you're looking for, because all I really have to offer right now is something super casual."

Sam watched as something behind Jordan's eyes seemed to shutter, a distance appearing between their close bodies.

"Oh," Jordan said.

"Oh?"

"I mean, that's totally fair, I understand needing some more time to heal, but I'm not looking for anything casual. I'm looking for something real." She met Sam's eyes for a split second before turning her hardened gaze to look out the window.

"Well, I think casual *can* be real—"

"Not for me."

There was a long pause, Sam staring at Jordan's profile, willing her to turn back into the soft, sweet, funny woman she'd been getting to know. But there was only this icy, hard butch in her place.

"I take it you're not coming inside then?" Sam said in a joking voice, an attempt to lighten the suddenly tense mood.

"No, thank you. Happy Passover," Jordan said as she leaned over and opened Sam's door for her.

Sam made it into her apartment before the tears spilled down her cheeks.

"I'm so glad you took today off, Sam," Virginia said from across the kitchen. They were both putting parts of the brunch feast on platters while Ben flipped his latest attempt at a matzo pancake.

"Yeah, I was really planning ahead for hangovers. I thought I'd drink both nights, but glad I didn't last night. One, because I'm too old to drink two nights in a row, and, two, because then I got to experience rejection stone cold sober! So fun." She skewered a grape on a toothpick viciously as she remembered the feeling of Jordan leaning past her to open the truck door.

Her dreams had been dark and sluggish. Waves of syrupy darkness had pulled her in and thrown her out of sleep over and over. Each time she woke, she'd been more tangled in the sheets, her curly hair growing wilder. The velvety, smoky scent of Jordan seemed to cling to the corners of each dream that slipped out of grasp. She'd finally given up on sleeping at around five in the morning.

"I still don't understand what happened," Ben said over

his shoulder, his arm jumping around as he tried to pry the 'pancake' from the pan with a spatula.

"I was a big girl and stated my needs and she flat out told me what I wanted wasn't real. It's fine. We want different things, it's not going to work out. Good to know early on!"

"I still think you should give her a call and ask for an explanation," Virginia said for the third time that morning as she mixed two different fruit juices into an oblong pitcher.

"Two nights in a row of false starts is really enough. Why force something?" Sam retorted as she finished the last fruit skewer. "This is a lot of food for the five of us."

"Ok, but the two of you follow each other around the room with your eyes. If that's not chemistry, what is?" Virginia replied in a dreamy voice. "And leftovers are a mom's best friend."

"It's just lust," Sam countered, even while some small voice in her head called her a liar. "By the way, did Leo and Alyssa tell you about their kids' school?"

"Oh yeah, thanks. I mean, we looked at that school and it's not a right fit, but they had some great intel on some playgroups and afterschool programs for Black children *and* we talked about approaching Temple Sinai's new rabbi about starting a monthly group for Jewish kids of color." Virginia brought her pitcher and trays over to where Sam was carefully stacking fruit skewers.

"And Leo is taking me golfing, which feels like a real potential friend moment," Ben added, turning away from the stove just in time to catch the eyes the two women were making at each other about golf.

The adults joined the twins at the long dining room table where they were coloring and laid out the brunch spread before Sam and Ben served the girls on matching princess plates.

"Is your boss still seeing that hot, shirtless dude on her

laptop background?" Virginia asked, taking a generous helping of Ben's pancake creation and sending him a loving smile.

"I think they're actually getting really serious. She's planning a vacation with him to Puerto Rico next month. She also finally told me that he's fifteen years younger than her. You should have heard the voice she said it in, positively scandalous."

"Good for her," Ben said. "I'm younger than Gin, you know."

"By four months." Virginia laughed.

"You know, about last night, there was also just something infectious, being there in that group of gays, oh, and one straight person, who all love each other so much, like *so much*. I mean, Cara and T's love just shoots cupid arrows at every bystander. And, wow, did I tell you that Cara has been also seeing Josh and now they're all talking about maybe trying out a throuple situation?"

"Honey, I so vaguely know who any of these people are."

"I know no one and I'm so confused," Ben added as he sliced another banana into the girls' cereal bowls.

"What's a throuple?" Yael asked, swirling the banana bits into the bran and milk, watching her handiwork and not looking up once to see Sam's horrified face.

"Yeah, and maybe let's watch our words," Ben added.

"A throuple is a couple with three people, sweetie," Virginia said. Sam caught Ben rolling his eyes and they shared an indulgent smile. "And good for them, but shouldn't all of that make you *more* interested in pursuing this thing with Jordan, not less?"

"No! What I'm saying is all that energy is what led to us locked in a closet, not fate or anything else."

"Excuse, locked in where?" Ben asked, his eyebrows coming dangerously close to disappearing into his hairline.

"Never mind, some other time in different company," Sam muttered with a glance at the kids.

"We're company," Gabi said to Yael and both of them dissolved into laughter and twinspeak.

"Your kids are too smart," Sam said, before adding, "And too cute. I'm glad they're still speaking their own language."

"Oh yeah, us too." Virginia's tone suggested the exact opposite.

"Plus, do I even stand a chance? Or is she just going to smush my little heart like a grape under her heel?"

"Please, no wine metaphors, I have a kosher wine hangover still from my Mom's." Ben chugged his coffee as if to wash away the mistakes of two nights prior.

Chapter Nine

She heard the answering machine start up, "Hi, you've reached Samantha Bilik's phone. I'm not available at the moment. So, say what you need to say to a machine instead."

"Uh, hi, Sam. It's Jordan. Jordan Massachi. Jordan, the butch from an app you don't actually own. Uh, anyway—"

Sam sprinted across the house to grab the phone off the wall, "Jordan?"

"What? Hi. How did you do that?"

"Do what?"

"Answer the phone while I was leaving you a voicemail?"

"Well you were actually talking to my answering machine, not my voicemail box."

There was a long silence. "Like a real answering machine? Those still work? What, did I call 1999?"

Sam let herself giggle into the receiver but mentally chastised herself when she realized she was twirling the phone cord around her finger too. "I'm even talking to you on a corded phone."

"Who are you? Is this like a hipster thing I'm too old to understand or are you actually my grandmother?"

"Ok, wow, wait a minute. One, you're not that much older than me. What are you, 35?"

"43."

Sam deposited that in the, "wow, must think about that and why it's so hot" mental bank for later.

"Ok, whatever. And two, my ex had a real thing about being super reachable all the time."

"Is she a spy?"

"Ha! No, she was an OB/GYN."

"Oh, I'm so sorry, I didn't realize."

"That I used to be with a doctor? Yeah, a real bummer."

"No, that your ex had passed away."

Now it was Sam's turn to pause for a moment. "What are you talking about?"

"Or, oh my god, sorry, was she just fired? You said 'she was a doctor,' not *is* a doctor."

"Oh wow, I mean, I think she's probably still a doctor, and she's definitely still alive. I see her very pregnant wife way too often to not know if she was dead."

"This is the 'wood' misunderstanding all over again." Jordan laughed. "But, wait, why do you see her wife?" Jordan sounded genuinely confused on the other end of the line and Sam wished she could see the shapes her perfect brows were stretching themselves into in confusion. "Is this one of those best-friends-with-my-exes-and-their-exes lesbian things?"

"No, no, *no*. Not at all. Actually, she's my rabbi's daughter, so I see her whenever I make myself go to services. Which isn't like super often, to be honest, but isn't *never*. And like, I thought about switching temples after it all went down, but that felt like she would win then. But I still think maybe I should. I mean, maybe I'd go more often if I did, and my rabbi can't even look me in the eyes anymore. I mean, it was just really ironic. My ex is a fertility specialist and Anna, my rabbi's daughter, was having some trouble conceiving with her husband, so I referred her to my ex. They'd never met because my ex was like allergic to her own Judaism. And then three months later, Anna was pregnant with donor sperm and leaving her husband and I came home to the two of them packing up all of my ex's stuff and—"

"Sam."

"Yeah?"

"Breathe. You're talking at warp speed."

She did, taking a long, shaky breath and placing a hand on the wall next to the phone. "Jordan, I'm so sorry. That was such a monologue. I just get so in my head about that stuff."

"You don't need to apologize." She paused for a second. "But, Sam?"

Nervously she responded, "Yes?"

"That story is fucking wild."

Both of them broke into relieved, overwhelmed laughter. Sam let herself fall a bit into the sound of Jordan's raspy sounds of joy.

"Yeah. It is. So, why are you calling me if not to hear me rant about an ex? And why do you have my house phone number?"

"Well, you can thank our matchmaker for the second thing. She gave me like three numbers for you, but didn't specify which one to use. This was the first on the list."

Silently, Sam both thanked and cursed Virginia for her meddling ways.

"I'm calling because I hate how we left things yesterday. And you still haven't made use of my cell phone number. I considered waiting, but I really hate games. You said something about just wanting a fling and I spooked. I'm not looking for something casual, that's not what kind of woman I am. But I thought about you all night and this morning realized I couldn't write you off that easily. And I'm sorry I was kind of a dick."

"You thought about me all night?"

A moment's hesitation before Jordan's response came, a bit hoarser than before, "I did."

"What did you think about?"

Again, another moment of silence. Sam imagined Jordan was weighing her options. Flirting could definitely still be just-a-fling behavior, but finally, "I thought about you in those dresses you wear."

"What kind of dresses are those?"

"The kind that taunt me with just bits of your thighs. That look like they want to be shoved up to your waist and held in one hand while I explore below them with the other."

"And here I thought they were called A-line dresses." Sam teased, her voice light, even though she felt heat shoot through her. How many times since Jordan had placed a hand on her leg had she imagined something very similar to what was being described now?

"Whatever they're called, they make me think about your ass constantly."

"What about my ass?"

"Well, what about mine?" Jordan's voice had gone from husky to suddenly laughing.

Sam realized she had been pressing her hip hard against the wall, the thrumming in her body almost unbearable. But Jordan's laughter pulled her back into the room.

"What about it?"

"You think I don't recognize you? Didn't you catch my joke at your seder?"

The flush that had been heating her chest with desire shot up to her face in embarrassment.

"Uh..."

"How you just stared at my back shamelessly at the crack of dawn when I was a total stranger at a bus stop? And I doubt you were admiring my belt."

"Why didn't you say anything before now?" Sam groaned and covered her face with a hand, trying to smooth down her mortification.

"I worried you wouldn't remember, maybe you're constantly staring at people's butts on the street and I was no one special to you. I also wanted to keep that moment for myself. I've thought about it often over the last several days."

"Why?"

"I imagine that I had taken advantage of the moment instead of letting you run off."

And they were suddenly back into very sexy territory. Sam remembered her resolve to match Jordan's confidence. "What would you have done?"

"When you jumped up, I would have pushed you back against the bus stop. Looked down that t-shirt to see how far down your blush went. I would have told you to go ahead and grab it if you were going to look at it like that."

"I would have just died right there."

"What were you thinking about before I caught you, Sam?"

A thrill shot through her at the deep tones of her own name.

"I was thinking about how I wanted to sink my teeth into it."

An ungodly sound came from the other end of the line.

"Sam." Her name was almost a whine on the other woman's lips. "I need to see you. Come over for the third night of Passover?"

"I can't make it through a third seder in a row, and that's not a thing." Sam laughed, half nerves, half pure want.

"It is a thing. It's a thing where there's absolutely no matzo and I get to *really* discover what's underneath those dresses and you get to do whatever you want to my ass."

Sam bit her lip hard to prevent herself from moaning like the wanton woman she'd become into the phone.

"Ok. When?"

"How about now?"

"Yes."

It wasn't until she was in a rideshare, blaring Fleetwood Mac in her headphones, on her way to Jordan's that she remembered the other woman's words about wanting something real. Her heart sank knowing she could only commit to casual. So she focused on the promise of Jordan's ass and "whatever she wanted." They could talk feelings after the fucking.

Chapter Ten

Sam met Jordan at the shop she owned and ran mostly alone. She was closing up for the day, talking on a final call confirming the next day's orders, and she winked at Sam as the bells above the door chimed with her entrance. Immediately she felt the blush of the two nights prior rush back up her neck and cheeks, so she turned away from Jordan to look around the store.

The front half was arranged for clients' perusal, binders full of photos from previous projects and some ready-made furniture with price tags that caused Sam's eyebrows to shoot up. Behind the furniture was a wall of sorts, made from beautifully hand carved wooden folding screens. Sticking her head in the doorway created by the gap between two of them, she looked around at the stacks of raw wood, table saws, and other machinery she didn't know the names for. If she hadn't already been practically soaking wet with desire, this would have tipped her over the edge. There is nothing hotter than a talented woman, Sam thought to herself.

"My office is all the way in the back." Jordan's voice came

from much closer to her than she expected and she whipped around to find her just arm's length away.

"Oh, yeah, great, perfect," Sam babbled as she told her heart to calm down. "I didn't hear you walking, so stealthy."

"Yeah, that's me, a regular Pink Panther," Jordan replied as she walked over to lock the door.

"Pink Panther? You *are* old."

Jordan snorted a laugh before returning to Sam, sliding her hands along the sides of the shorter woman's dress, and leaning in to place the gentlest kiss on her lips. Pulling slightly back she whispered against her mouth, "Not too old to rock your world."

Sam groaned at the cheesy comment even while she felt her legs turn to hot liquid. Jordan used her grip to turn Sam and safely navigate her through all of the shop's equipment to the back room. There was a beautiful dark wood desk, as well as a low light brown leather couch arranged with two intricately carved high back wooden chairs.

"Did you build this desk?"

"Yes, and now I'm going to fuck you on it."

A thrill shot up Sam's spine at the words, and again as Jordan spun her around and lifted her onto the desk surface. *Wow, she's strong,* Sam awed and reached out to grip the biceps that had effortlessly picked her up. Jordan's hands pulled her knees wide, coming close to stand between them and she leaned in to speak gently into Sam's ear, "I'm going to make you come over and over until you beg me to stop."

In enthusiastic agreement, Sam brought her mouth to the neck before her, her hands quickly unbuttoning and removing the crisp button-up, leaving only a tight sports bra. Jordan's breath stumbled when Sam nipped at her neck, Sam reaching down to slide her palm along the front of the standing woman's pants. Her fingers moved over a hard cock encased in jeans, and let her teeth sink into Jordan's neck a little harder, earning her an almost animalistic growl. Her fingers were swift as she undid the belt buckle, and shoved the jeans as far down as she could reach.

The silicone dick snapped to attention, now freed from its constraint and Sam broke away from the path she'd been mapping down Jordan's shoulder with her mouth to watch her own hand smooth over the shaft and trail along the tip. It was close to Jordan's skin color with realistic looking veins creating enticing ridges along its length.

While she took in this welcome surprise, Jordan's hands had worked their way up her thighs, far under her skirt, meeting the crease of stomach and leg. "I love your thighs," the butch woman moaned throatily into Sam's hair, leaning toward her, pushing her cock against the seated woman's core. Sam moaned and lifted her legs to wrap around Jordan's hips, grinding against the firm erection. For long, delicious moments they dry humped like teenagers in the back of a borrowed car, Sam panting Jordan's name as the thrusting woman pressed teeth and tongue against the throbbing pulse in her neck. *I'll have to wear a turtleneck tomorrow*, Sam thought with wicked pleasure.

Eventually, Jordan reached beneath her skirts, pushed her soft cotton panties aside, and slid strong, rough fingers through her slickened folds. Sam felt herself convulse at the touch, already so close to coming. And when Jordan pushed two long fingers inside of her she screamed with need and bliss and sweet aching. Her thumb circled Sam's clit while her fingers stroked over and over inside of her Sam wrapped her arms around Jordan's back wanting her closer, wanting more of her. She knew she was riding Jordan's hand shamelessly, her hips rising off the desk and slapping back down against the dark wood in an erratic pattern.

The combination of sensations pushed her over the edge.

Sam arched her back hard, her hair spilling over the other side of the desk, the room disappearing around her.

She pulled herself up, murmuring soft, nonsensical words, meeting the other woman's eyes, which blazed with endless need. Before Sam could even reach the cock, and below it, Jordan sucked her fingers clean before trailing them against Sam's own mouth. As she took them between her lips, Jordan pushed the length of her cock into Sam's pussy, both of them crying out. The overwhelming proximity was both too much and not enough for each woman. Jordan pulled their bodies tightly together so with each thrust she rubbed roughly against the bundle of nerves at the top of Sam's opening. Sam gripped Jordan's ass with bruising pressure and Jordan returned the painful pleasure in her own hold on Sam's waist.

They rocked their hips toward and away from one another in sync, faster and faster until Sam cried out once more. While she was still riding the waves of her orgasm, Jordan pulled her off of the desk, turning her over so her stomach and diamond hard nipples pushed against the wood. Steady hands slid her underwear off her legs, and squeezed the back of her thighs, spreading her obscenely to the audible pleasure of the woman behind her. Sam panted, still catching her breath from the frantic pace they'd made together, and felt an illicit thrill knowing Jordan was just watching her. After another moment she wiggled her hips and immediately felt the press of the cock head between her swollen lips.

Jordan moved into her urgently, her fingers clutching at exposed hips as if she might just slip away. Her thumbs pressing into the dimples of her ass as Sam's hips rolled. The voice of concern that seemed to always be whispering in the back of Sam's head disappeared, the only things that mattered was keeping her grip on the edge of the desk, the feeling of the fingers anchoring her to the wood, and the rhythm of the cock pushing into her.

Something about the press of the body against her own, the tenderness of the voice moaning her name told her this was anything but casual. That both of them would have their hearts ripped out when this was over, but that was then.

Jordan's fingers slipped below her to circle into her and it took only seconds for her to find the crest of sensation, to ride the wave of rushing heat that threatened to burn her up with its intensity. Sam heard herself cry out Jordan's name as she clenched around her for a third time, before her body fell limp against the desk below her.

* * *

The next several days flew by in a blur of flirty texts and frantic hookups, intermixed with work and fantasizing.

After Sam had recovered from the back office fucking, Jordan had taken her upstairs to her apartment, to cuddle with her on her immaculately made bed. They'd both dozed off for a while, before sweetly waking each other up with slow kisses and lazily roaming hands. It had led to a fourth orgasm, brought on by painfully slow stroking and the whispering of sweet nothings.

Somehow Sam had found the strength to head home, they both had early mornings. Once in her apartment, she dug Jordan's number out of her trash and added it to her phone. That night, just before falling asleep, Sam texted her, "I never got to do WHATEVER I WANTED to your ass."

She woke to her alarm and a mirror photo from Jordan of the butch's firmly toned butt, her jeans pulled just below the cheeks. "This ass?"

Sam groaned, turning to bite her pillow in need. She masturbated quickly, sent back an extremely unlike-her photo of her hand down her pajama bottoms and got ready for work.

All day long they texted about asses, Jordan sending

photos of donkeys in clothes, Sam responding with the politicians and movie stars who were the biggest jerks. Both of them sent lists of euphemisms for butts—Sam's favorite was tushy, Jordan's was derriere. When the work day was almost over, Jordan asked, "Can I come over tonight?"

And Sam arrived home to Jordan on her front steps with matzo pizza supplies and the bottle of whisky from the seder. They ate and drank and broke into the matzo toffee that Sam had forgotten to bring to Cara and T's. The unfurling of warmth in her chest was definitely from the whisky. *It's not about Jordan*, Sam knowingly lied to herself, *nothing to do with the thrill of four days in a row of time spent together, of her smoky wood scent, and the paths her rich brown eyes were marking across her body*. Yet she could feel the constant smile on her lips, and the tug of her heart every time Jordan smiled in return.

That night Jordan made her come so many times she lost count, and every time she attempted to return the favor, Jordan would kiss her silly and make her come again.

The next day they woke up together, took a shower together where Jordan knelt before her and made her come in her mouth. And spent another work day deliriously texting and smiling like a fool at her colleagues.

"I can't come over tonight."

"Who said you're invited?"

"The moans you made in the shower this morning did."

"You rake!"

"Your neighbors will be happy to get a night's sleep tho."

"Are you too busy with a woodmergency to finally let me put my mouth on you?"

"Now who's the rake? No, friend's bachelor party, we're going bar hopping."

Which is how Sam found herself spending a quiet night in, masturbating to yet more selfies of Jordan. These were drunk texts from the bar bathrooms. In one it was just a shot of her belt undone, which was enough to set Sam's core aflame. *Oh man, I have it bad*, she lamented even while stripping down and sliding under the sheets. In another, with a different bathroom wall behind her, there was a shot of her cock in her hand, a different one than the one from the day in the shop. A moment later a short video of her pumping it, the sound of her moans a perfect soundtrack to Sam's own activities.

She'd never dated a woman who'd so casually worn strap-ons before. In fact, she could only ever remember using strap-ons once during sex before meeting Jordan. She found that she loved it, loved the confidence with which Jordan went about her life with a constant erection, evident through her pants if you knew where to look. She knew she needed to put some more space between them, could feel her heart getting in too deep, but that could wait.

She woke, her hand still between her legs, to a text at 1am, "2 late to cum over?"

"Plz 'cum' over."

Immediately there was a knock at the door and she answered it stark naked. Jordan took a long look at her before shutting the door behind her and wordlessly pushing Sam up against the wall. She tasted sweet and smoky, whisky on her lips. Her hands played over Sam's nipples until she was begging for more. Jordan responded by grabbing both of her wrists in one hand, holding them against the wall above Sam's head, and continuing to slowly trail her fingers around the sensitive buds. Finally, when Sam was gasping with need, Jordan freed her cock and slid easily into Sam's soaking entrance. She pulled one leg up onto her hip and drove into the naked woman until Sam was sobbing into Jordan's neck. Only then did Jordan release her hands, pull Sam's other leg up around her and walk them to the bed where they slowly moved against each other until sleep over-took them.

* * *

"Can we go to dinner tonight?" Jordan asked, eyes still shut, as Sam slipped from the bed to start the day.

"Oh, good morning." Sam padded into the bathroom to start the shower and called back out into the room, "Sure. Where are you thinking?"

Jordan mumbled something Sam couldn't hear and she walked back into the room to ask again.

"I can't yell. Too much whisky. Mistakes," Jordan mumbled, eyes still shut. "A client told me about this matzo pop-up. Let's go. I want people to see you out on my arm."

"Like I'm a trophy wife?" Sam teased.

"Yeah, exactly that. My thirty year old trophy wife," Jordan teased back.

"Hey! That's still a lot younger than you."

"I take issue with 'a lot,' but point taken."

"Are you going to come shower?"

"No, I'm planning to die right here, thanks."

Sam realized that Jordan might want to stay in her apart-ment after she'd left for work and she felt an equal measure of affection and terror at the idea. Another look at Jordan's adorably messy hair and exhausted face tipped the scales toward affection.

Chapter Eleven

That night they met at the pop-up, which was really a food truck near park benches, and immediately Sam noticed Jordan was on edge. She waited until they'd ordered their food—she got another matzo pizza, Jordan ordered a precarious looking matzo sandwich—before asking what was wrong.

"Nothing, don't worry about it." Jordan put on a clearly forced smile and tried to bite into her sandwich. The matzo cracked into several pieces and everything spilled out onto the compostable plate, forcing her to eat it in bits and pieces with her fingers. Sam laughed and the mood lifted.

* * *

After dinner they got into Jordan's truck and Sam immediately sensed that the dark cloud had returned. They drove mostly in silence, all of her attempts at jokes and conversations falling flat. When they parked outside of Jordan's shop, Sam started to open her door before she realized the other woman still had her seatbelt on and was watching her with brows pulled tightly together.

"Jordan, come on, what is up?" Sam reached out to touch her forearm, but Jordan moved it away.

"Did you talk to Cara and T this week?"

"What? Yeah. Yesterday, we caught up a bit."

"What did you talk about?"

"Why are you asking about this? Why does my conversation with them matter?" Sam felt an icy sense of foreboding all along her spine.

"Well, T called me today and was really surprised when I told them we'd spent the whole week together and were seeing each other again tonight."

"Yeah, I didn't tell them about that. I'm sorry, was I supposed to?" Sam couldn't keep the edge of irritation out of her voice.

"I mean, we have seen each other every single day, and they are two of your best friends. Don't you think that's kind of weird?"

"No, I don't. I told you I wanted something casual." Sam turned her body, her back was fully against the door so she could look at Jordan straight on. "And so yeah, I wanted to keep this between us while I figure out how to keep this casual."

"And I am trying to let you take your time, but this isn't casual, Sam. I don't care that it's only been a few days. The way I feel around you, the way I feel inside of you, that isn't casual."

Jordan wouldn't make eye contact with her, and her voice sounded dull, like she'd already seen where this conversation went and was protecting herself from its outcome.

"Well, this way you're acting only makes me feel more certain that this should just be a temporary thing."

"Ok, Sam," Jordan said flatly and was out of her seatbelt and the car in a breath. Sam sat blinking back tears in the passenger seat before following her toward the building.

"Jordan!" She called as the other woman reached the front door. The figure in front of her stalled for a second, and half turned back to her. "Come on, what is going on? We just started seeing each other. Why are you so hurt?"

"I don't want to fight on the street, come inside," she replied, leading them both up to the apartment above the shop.

Sam sat in the chair closest to the door, but Jordan walked past the seating area to open a window. She stood, staring out at the street for a minute, seeming to be gathering her strength, before she turned back to face Sam.

"Look, you told me about all of your ex drama, and I didn't return the favor." A sad smile twisted on Jordan's lips. "This is all bringing some of that trauma back up for me. Like I told you, we just finalized our divorce last year, and even though we were over a long time before that, I'm still working through some shit."

"Ok, so tell me about it."

"I thought you just wanted this to be casual? Why would I share all of this bullshit with a fling?"

Sam's sharp intake of breath revealed a lot to both of them about just how casual this all wasn't, but Sam wasn't ready to investigate that.

"Tell me," Sam managed around a growing lump in her throat. "I'm trying, but I need you to tell me."

Jordan remained standing, propping a fist against the window frame above her head, leaning the side of her firm body against the wood. Her normally sparkling eyes were remote and glossy, the corners of her soft mouth pulled tightly downward. Sam thought about the 80's vampire movie Gin had made her watch the last time they'd had a friend sleepover, the way the forever-teenage boys would brood and lean against every door frame. She would have laughed if not for the massive weight on her chest. She inwardly chided herself for such an inappropriate thought in such a moment.

"I don't know if she ever loved me, really. We met when we were both so young and neither of us knew what we wanted out of life. But I knew I wanted her. She was so bright, luminous. She wasn't out yet, but I was okay being her secret for a lot longer than I think I should have let myself be." Jordan turned her body to rest her shoulders against the window and run both hands down her face. "It just created this weird power thing between us. And, if I'm being totally honest with you, it was really fucking hot. Knowing that while all the men in her life flirted with her, I was the one taking her home."

Sam felt the sudden surge of jealousy and pain rise up, but extinguished it with one look at Jordan's tortured expression. "How long were you two together in secret?"

"Well, by the time she was finally ready to tell her family and friends, we'd been married for a year. We'd been dating on and off for almost two decades. Most of our thirties were spent apart, she tried to make it work with this guy, this friend of the family, but of course it didn't work out. So, she came back and I was seeing someone, but when Monica was still in the picture I was never really serious about anyone else. I was always just waiting for her to come back."

"Decades?" It came out as more of a squeak than a word.

"Yes. I would have followed her anywhere, it was a really unhealthy situation. And I think that's what ended up causing all of the problems with her family, not just that she was gay, but that she hadn't trusted them enough to tell them before she got married without them knowing."

Jordan's stance didn't change, but Sam sensed a tightening, like the pressure in the air before a thunderstorm. "Except her family loves her a lot, so instead they directed all of that anger my direction. And they were right, in some ways. They'd known me as Monica's best friend, had never questioned why

I was always around. And I let them believe it was just that deep. I went pretty far out of my way actually to keep that up. Her sister stopped by our apartment once unexpectedly and I faked a stomach virus to keep her from coming in and seeing all of the photos I couldn't hide in time."

Jordan couldn't conceal the bitterness in her voice anymore, it laced each word even as her mouth twisted into a shadow of a smile. Sam desperately wanted to stand up and touch her, but she knew she couldn't, not while they were still at odds about what they wanted. "We tried to make it work for many, many more years, but I wasn't welcome in her family's home anymore and she started spending more and more time with them attempting to mend fences. It became unbearable, it felt like I was a secret all over again."

Even from where Sam was sitting across the room, she could see Jordan's eyes line with tears. She pushed up out of her chair, unable to resist comforting the vulnerable woman pouring her heart out any longer. She wrapped her arms around Jordan, felt the chill from the window seeping into the other woman's back and pressed their bodies firmly together, trying to push some of her warmth across the barrier of their clothes. For several agonizing moments, Jordan's arms remained stiffly at her sides before finally tightening around Sam's waist.

"Jordan." Sam moved her hands up her back to rest on firm shoulders. "You don't deserve to be hidden. You're an incredible person, I'm glad you freed yourself from that."

Jordan stiffened against her, gripping Sam's wrists and pushing some space between their bodies. "I didn't. She left me. She said she couldn't keep living with a reminder of her mistakes."

Sam grabbed hold of the butch's belt, Jordan's fingers still encircling her wrists, pulling her close once more. "Either way, you deserve to be celebrated."

"But not by you, right? This is just a casual thing, right?" There was sadness in her voice, and just a suggestion of frustration.

Sam started to pull herself away, but Jordan's grip tightened on her wrists as she closed her teeth over Sam's bottom lip. They fell against each other, their mouths hungry and insistent. Jordan nipped sharply at the edges of her mouth between sweeps of her tongue. And yet there was something gentle about it, almost reverent. Sam slid her hand from Jordan's belt loop into rough jeans, smoothing her palms over the cotton briefs, cupping the firm ass. Jordan growled into her mouth as she tried to turn their bodies, but Sam stayed firm in her stance, pushing the other woman roughly against the window.

"Sam—"

"Shh. Let me take care of you."

With suddenly shaky hands she unbuttoned Jordan's shirt, sliding it off of her muscular shoulders, leaving it on at the wrists, trapping some of Jordan's nervous energy. She flattened her palms on Jordan's upper chest, leaning in to gently bite at the skin where neck met shoulder. She heard Jordan's small gasp and grinned against the woman's shoulder. Then she leaned back, trailing her fingers down past the tight sports bra flattening what little chest was there, to rest just at the edge of torso and pants.

In just a few days, they'd already seen each other naked more times than she could currently count through the haze of intense desire. Each time had felt charged with something so beyond lust, yet she felt like she was seeing Jordan clearly for the first time now. Vulnerable, strong. Sam felt the lump in her throat again as she took in the other woman's masculine beauty.

She knelt in front of this gorgeous being and licked a teasing line from hip bone to hip bone. She wanted to kiss, lick, and bite every single inch of Jordan's skin. She wanted to worship her body the way Jordan had been worshiping hers for the last week.

Jordan groaned and pushed her hips towards Sam. "You're killing me."

"Patience is a virtue." Sam laughed as she took the corner of the jean's fabric in her mouth.

"Who the fuck told you that?" She tried to free her hands of the tangled shirt, but Sam reached out and held them against the wall by the wrist.

Feeling a rush of nerves met by a wave of pure need, Sam met Jordan's eyes and then tugged the jeans with her teeth, unbuttoning the closure. Jordan moaned again and let her head fall back against the wall.

Sam let go of Jordan's wrists just long enough to undo the zipper and work both pants and briefs totally off. Jordan managed to free herself of her shirt in that time, and her hands tangled into Sam's hair just as the kneeling woman's mouth met the juncture of thigh and torso.

Sam teased her way from thigh to thigh, before finally slowly slipping her tongue into Jordan's folds. She heard her hiss and felt her fingers tighten painfully in her hair. The sharp sensation against her scalp only heightened her own growing arousal.

"No surprise cock today, I see."

"I wasn't planning on fucking you today." Jordan met her eyes and Sam saw twin pools of aching hunger there.

"Too bad, I was really looking forward to sucking your dick," she purred before tracing her fingers along Jordan's folds and spreading them wide.

"Don't worry sweetheart, I plan on having many chances for you to suck me off in the future." Sam's heart did a funny flop at the mention of their future, but before she could think too much about it, Jordan was pulling her hair again. "Why don't you give me a preview of what that mouth can do right now?"

Sam felt her face heat, and turned her attention to Jordan's clit, dancing her tongue on either side of the ridge, slowly licking the full length revealed before her. Jordan's hands tugged and gripped her head, as she moaned directions and pet names and dirty words. She loved being here, kneeling in front of this sweet, powerful woman, feeling both in control and controlled. She breathed in the sweet, smoky scent of the butch before her as she ravenously licked and sucked.

She traced one finger around the edge of Jordan's opening, seeking permission, all of this new and nerve-wracking, and causing her to press her thighs together to keep from begging to be fucked right there.

Jordan granted permission by swinging her thigh onto Sam's shoulder and pulling her in even closer. Sam slipped her tongue deeply into Jordan, savoring the feeling of the standing woman shivering with pleasure against her mouth. As she took control, directing the tempo and direction of the movements, she rubbed her thumb over Jordan's clit, speeding her towards the loss of control she so desperately needed.

Hips bucking in increasingly erratic patterns, Jordan was panting for breath, gripping the curly hair in her hands as much for pain and pleasure as to keep her balance. "Touch yourself."

As if she'd been waiting for permission, Sam's free hand immediately shot under her skirt to the damp skin there, sliding under the panties she'd carefully picked hoping Jordan would tear them from her body. Instead she hadn't even been able to show them off yet and they were already close to soaking.

She barely needed to rub her own center of nerves before she was moaning, sending vibrations straight into Jordan's core.

"Oh fuck, Sam, I'm so close. Come with me, come with me, baby."

Sam moaned deep and loud as she fucked Jordan with her tongue, her own pleasure finding its peak.

Jordan's thigh tightened on Sam's shoulder, her hands holding her in place while the butch ground against her tongue, shaking as waves of ecstasy poured over them both.

For several moments the only sound was of the two women attempting to catch their breath. Finally, Jordan slid her leg off of Sam, disentangled her fingers from the mussed curls, and cleared her throat.

Sam felt a sliver of fear that this was the moment Jordan would deliver the ultimatum—a relationship or nothing at all. She steeled herself for the next words.

"Go get my cock."

Her eyes shot up to find the dark look staring down at her. Surprise and relief caused her to laugh. "What?"

Jordan held Sam's chin in one hand, and slid two fingers into Sam's mouth with the other. "You said you wanted to suck my dick. I want to see what a good girl you can be. You look so pretty on your knees. And I want to give you a taste of what you're missing by putting an expiration date on us."

Sam tried to push back and say that was unfair, but Jordan slipped her fingers deeper into her mouth, almost causing her to gag, which, paired with the forcefulness and dirty words just uttered, caused a new rush of need.

She closed her lips over the fingers and sucked them in deep, sliding her tongue over the rough lines of them. She allowed herself to fall completely into the moment, moaning and Jordan began to slowly thrust them in and out of her throat.

Then they were gone and Sam opened her eyes again to find want and need and sadness starting down at her. "Go get my cock, it's on the dresser, and come back so you can show me everything that mouth can do."

Sam was sure she'd never moved so quickly in her life, and still when she came back into the room, Jordan had somehow redressed, though she'd left the shirt open over her taut abs, and sat herself on the leather loveseat.

"Kneel here." Jordan patted the cushion next to her. Sam quickly complied as the other woman took the dildo from her and fed it through the open fly in her pants. As soon as it was secure, Sam set upon it with tongue and lips. Jordan once again threaded fingers through her hair, but this time only her right hand. Her left hand slid up Sam's thighs, over the curve of her ass, pooling her skirt around her waist. She felt incredibly exposed. She felt terrified and safe, hopeful and hopeless. Her stomach and heart were all tied up together. The amount of warmth and trust she felt for this other woman was a giant wave crashing down around her and she was certain she'd drown if she gave into it.

Chapter Twelve

Sam's head rested on Jordan's shoulder, both of them somehow mostly dressed, yet fully bare to one another for the first time. She traced her fingertips along the lines of Jordan's muscles and breathed in her alluring smell. She never wanted this moment to end, and knew once either of them broke the silence that would be the end of not just this vulnerability, but possibly their time together. Jordan, as usual, found her courage first.

"Sam, we need to talk about what we're doing."

Sam buried her face in Jordan's armpit and made a sound a lot like a broken motor attempting to start.

"That's one way of putting it." Jordan's laugh was obviously half hearted and they both let it linger in the room until Sam found her voice.

"I love what we're doing. I haven't felt this good since—" She trailed off, trying to remember a time when spending every free moment with another person felt energizing instead of exhausting. She gave up after a minute. "For a really, really long time. I don't want this to end. But I also am so afraid, Jordan."

The other woman smoothed her palm along Sam's back as she spoke, soothing her, making a small piece of her hope that she would talk sense into her, make her believe that a relationship was possible, even while the volume of her doubt rose up to drown out that hope.

"This isn't just sex for me," Jordan said. "And I don't want it to be. But I can't just have sex with you, there's too much here. I want all of it."

"It's not just sex for me either," Sam reassured her. "I mean, the sex is definitely some of the best of my life—" at this Jordan made something dangerously close to a gloating sound and Sam rolled her eyes before adding, "if not *the* best sex of my life, but that's not what distracts me at work or keeps me up for hours smiling after we've parted. It's all of the other things. That's what's fucking terrifying."

"For me, too," Jordan agreed. "The good parts and the fear, but it's worth it, Sam. Being afraid and learning to trust each other, it's worth it for what I know is happening."

"What do you know is happening?" Sam's mouth felt dry and she sat up to look down at Jordan, equally afraid and hopeful for the answer. Jordan joined her in sitting, reaching out and grabbing Sam's slightly trembling hands.

"I'm falling for you, isn't that obvious?" Jordan's eyes were pools of joy and warmth and Sam had to look away from them to prevent herself from slipping entirely, irretrievably into them. She found a spot on the wall behind her to fixate on instead, blinking back the tears she felt threatening to overwhelm her and the sudden lump in her throat.

"You can't. I can't." Sam shook her head, desperately trying to find the words that would stop this conversation without stopping their time together.

"I can't what? Fall for you? Or admit it to you?" Jordan's grasp on her hands tightened. "I know we're just getting to know each other, Sam, and all I'm asking is that you let us keep doing that. I'm not asking you to tell me you love me a week into knowing each other, but I'd be dishonest if I didn't tell you that I know we're on that path." Suddenly her eyes clouded, "At least for me. But if you're feeling differently—"

"It's not that," Sam forced out, feeling the tears win their escape and slip down her cheeks. She pulled one hand from Jordan's hold to wipe them angrily away with the palm. "I mean, it is way too fast. I'm not that kind of person, I like to take my time, but that's not even it."

"What is it?" Jordan's voice was still a caress, but Sam could sense a wall going up behind the words.

"You said it, learning to trust each other. And I just don't know how to do that. You've already told me that all women are just a placeholder for you."

"What?" Jordan's hands went limp against her own, her eyes widened just the smallest bit.

Sam realized Jordan was right, they were on a dangerous path, already she could read this woman so well, knew when her moods were changing and could feel her fear. She couldn't let this go on, not with another person who might crush her heart, she needed something safe. She could end this now, before either of them had completely fallen for the other and they'd both recover, they'd have the story of their spring fling, their Passover romance, and both be able to move on with their own lives.

How had Virginia crassly put it? She needed to clear out the cobwebs? Well, those had certainly been swept away. She felt totally hollowed out. Yes, it was the right decision to help them both move forward, but first she needed to say the words, to get Jordan to see her side of things.

"You told me that all other women can't compare to Monica." Sam watched Jordan wince at Monica's name and knew she was making the right decision. "That you could never really be serious about anyone else because you are always waiting for her to come back. I can't be a placeholder, Jordan."

"No one is asking you to do that." Now there was an edge of anger in Jordan's voice. She pulled her hands back, crossing her arms over her body, shuttering her eyes to Sam. "I told you that Monica and I are over for good. And I'm not waiting for her, I've moved on with my life. It's you who can't get over being left."

The air went out of Sam and she felt like she'd been punched in the stomach. Of course it was true, and she'd basically said as much just a moment ago, but the icy cold tone of Jordan's words was unexpectedly devastating.

"I don't think anyone should have to get over being betrayed, Jordan." Sam poured the pain she was feeling into her voice as she said the other woman's name. "And yes, maybe I don't want to get stabbed in the back again, so why would I put myself in a situation that would guarantee a repeat of that trauma?"

"Sam, you're just trying to push me away. Which doesn't feel great, by the way." Jordan's eyes gentled and Sam made herself look away once again, afraid of letting herself soften as well. "Let's try this again. Yes, we're moving too fast, but we can slow things down. Let me take you on a real date. Let's pretend we actually did meet on that app, or that I'd asked you out at that bus stop. Don't give up before we've even tried. I can't promise I'm never going to hurt you, people hurt each other everyday. This conversation has basically thrown my heart into a blender."

She reached back out and took Sam's hands in one of her own, reaching up with the other to gently wipe away the tears Sam hadn't realized were still streaming down her face. "But I can promise that I will never betray you. I was a different person when I was with Monica, or the same person but I hadn't learned my lesson yet. I'm a real grown-up now."

Sam let out a little hiccuping laugh at this, a woman a decade older than her admitting to finally being an adult. She felt like she was standing at a crossroads, two different unknowable chasms before her. Then, disturbingly, she thought of her boss and her much younger shirtless boyfriend. Her boss had been embarrassed, supposedly, to have accidentally screenshared that photo, but she had clearly also been proud. At the time, and when she'd joked to Gin about it, she'd thought her boss was proud of the fact that her lover was a Grade A hunk.

Now Sam wondered if her boss had been proud that she'd gotten over whatever hang-ups had kept her from staying in previous relationships long enough to make those guys her computer background.

Would she, Sam, also have to go through a series of painful short-term relationships to learn her own lessons? It felt like letting Pauline win again, not only had she cheated on her, left her, and was having a baby with someone else, but now Sam would be stuck having to learn to trust all over again because of it. It just didn't seem fair.

"Hello, Sam? Where did you go?" Jordan waved a hand jokingly in front of Sam's face. "I thought we were sitting here together, spilling our guts out to each other, but it's like you left the room entirely."

"I was thinking about my boss, actually," Sam admitted.

"Uh, what?" The adorably confused scrunched up brows were back on Jordan's face and Sam felt her heart give a painful lurch.

"It doesn't matter. It all comes down to trust, and I don't know if that's a thing that really grows with time or if it's like a chemistry thing where you have it or you don't."

"Of course it grows with time. Don't do this, don't cut us off because of my past mistakes, because I opened up to you." A landscape of pain and sadness rolled out between them.

"No, of course not. Thank you for sharing all of that with me." Sam squeezed Jordan's hands. "Please don't regret that. It's not about you, and I'm sorry I said the thing about being a placeholder. It's about me, and I'm just not ready to learn my own lesson. Before Pauline, I never got super serious about anyone. I didn't really try, to be honest. I wasn't interested in investing in those relationships. It's like in your early twenties, you're expected to just be having a good time and being casual, and then there's a switch that gets flipped and all of a sudden everyone around you is getting married to the partner you thought they were just having a good time with."

"And your switch didn't flip?"

"Well, I think what I'm realizing right now is that maybe I don't have one, and maybe no one has one. Your comment about being a grown-up now is connecting some dots for me. When all of the people around me started getting really serious about their futures, I was with Pauline. And it just felt like I might as well get really serious about her." Sam took a deep breath to steady herself, she felt rushes of hot and cold and knew her hands were still trembling. "But we never actually talked about it, I just started doubling down on our relationship and I'm the one who insisted we move in together. And I didn't think about the fact that she moved into my almost-affordable one bedroom apartment and rented out her condo, but didn't sell it. I just thought, oh, it's time to get on that marriage escalator, let's do it."

Jordan made a sympathetic face that unleashed more tears from Sam's watery eyes, and nodded along knowingly.

"So, yeah, she really fucked me over in the end, but did we actually build trust together before that? Did we actually build a life together? I'm realizing probably not, and that maybe I don't know how to build trust with another person at all."

"Let's learn it together. Let's learn how to trust and care

for each other in the ways we want to be trusted and cared for." Jordan hesitated for a second before adding, "And loved."

Sam let out a hiccuping sob, leaning forward and hiding her face in Jordan's open shirt. She knew her make-up was probably in streaks across her cheeks and that she'd leave mascara spots on the other woman's soft button-up, but she needed a moment of comfort before things came to a true end. Jordan, clearly thinking Sam had finally seen the light, let out a sigh of relief and wrapped her arms around Sam's back, pulling her close.

They stayed like that for several minutes before Sam's breathing had evened out and she'd composed her thoughts. Slowly, she pushed away from Jordan, swiped her thumps under her eyes to attempt to contain the makeup disaster, and broke both their hearts. "I can't, Jordan. I'm sorry."

The handsome, sweet, soft woman stayed sitting in the bed, watching Sam as she collected her belongings, shoving them erratically into different pockets of her purse, and straightening out her clothing and hair best she could. She still sat there as Sam mustered up the courage to meet her eyes. Jordan's face was wet with silent tears that caused Sam's stomach to constrict. She took a shaky breath, raised a hand to wave awkwardly goodbye, and made her way out the front door.

Once there she allowed herself to fall entirely to pieces until the tears stopped coming and she picked herself up from the wood floor of Jordan's hallway and made her way home.

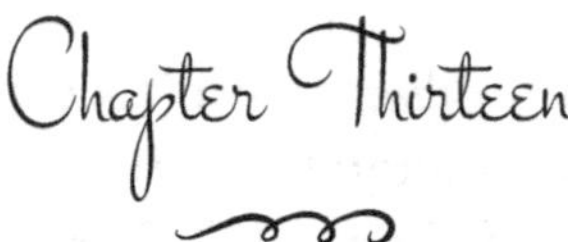

Chapter Thirteen

"What time are you going to be here, and are you bringing Jordan with you?" Virginia shouted at her phone from across the expanse of her kitchen.

"Gin, I can hear you perfectly fine, the speakerphone is doing its job, no need to blow your voice out." Sam gulped down some air, fighting back the tears that had come and gone in unpredictable waves all night. "And I'll be there in like an hour to help you prep, but there will be no Jordan. We're over."

"Oh, honey, what?" Virginia's voice was suddenly much closer to the phone. "What happened? Yesterday you just said you had a little fight. Did she end it over that? Did you go over there to fix things?"

"What the hell, Gin. Why are you assuming she ended things? And why do I have to be the one to fix them?"

"Sam, I'm sorry, you're right. You just sound so sad I didn't think it could be your decision."

"Well, it was. I'm not ready, and it's too dangerous."

They both let the silence spread for a while before Sam

said she had to go get ready and Virginia reminded her to bring dessert.

* * *

To help herself feel better, Sam put on her nicest dress: a thick, stiff cotton in hunter green that forced her to stand up straight instead of the shoulders-up-to-the-ears hunching she did all day at work. The structured cap sleeves and fitted bodice flowed into a full, knee-length skirt. It was her only dress without pockets, so she slipped on athletic shorts underneath to store her wallet and phone, and shoved down the thoughts of Jordan's hands on her thighs. She swiped on her usual mascara and two small blots of blush—*not that I've needed help blushing recently*—and decided to forego lipstick, knowing her favorite shade wouldn't last through four glasses of beverage.

She threw the dessert into a tupperware, and then sat on her couch to wait for her rideshare. She was growing to hate the quiet moments. It was when there was nothing else to listen to that she could most clearly hear Jordan's laughter, feel Jordan's hands on her thighs. She'd had a sex dream last night about Jordan's ass. And she woke up resentful that in all of their time in the bedroom, she'd never gotten to bite those cheeks.

The whole ride to the seder Sam kept opening her texts with Jordan and then immediately forcing herself to close them. She wanted to write to her. Wanted to try again, but the fear was blinding. Obviously, she wasn't ready.

"Samantha!" Virginia greeted her at the door in a floor length, sleeveless floral dress, her hair mostly elegant in a sweeping updo except for the excessive number of butterfly clips the girls had obviously contributed to the look. Her best friend pulled her into a hug, gently rubbing her hands along Sam's back and making motherly soothing sounds.

"I'm not crying, Gin." Sam said indignantly from within her embrace.

"Yeah, but you can if you need to, honey," she murmured soothingly, still rubbing her hands on her back.

"Ok, ok, knock it off," Sam said, pushing away from her friend. "What still needs to be done?"

Virginia led her into the house, pointing out the things that needed to be put on trays, or sliced, or poured. They worked side by side in silence for a while before Sam asked, "Where is everyone?"

"Ben is playing with the girls. Our bargain for them doing yet another seder was that he had to play Pretty Princess with them for an hour."

"Ugh, he's the prettiest princess."

"Yes. Yes, he is." Virginia tried to keep her voice level as she asked, "So, honey. Are you going to try again with Jordan? What happened?"

"I don't know if I can. I'm so fucking scared."

"Of what?"

"Of everything Pauline did to me happening again."

"Honey, you can't avoid getting hurt for the rest of your life. You love being in love!" Virginia turned to face her. "But I can promise that no one else is going to leave you after they get a patient pregnant."

Sam didn't realize she had started crying until she laughed. "Yeah, that's probably true."

"And Jordan doesn't even have patients. Plus, she's already giving wood to everyone coming into her shop."

"The wood jokes really are endless."

"They are."

Ben came into the room then, saw the tears drying on

Sam's face and pulled her in for a wordless hug. He rocked her a few times before Sam objected.

"You two, I don't need another set of parents!"

"Just habit at this point." Ben shrugged. "Ok, let's get this seder on the road."

They all carried the seder plates and dishes out to the table and Ben went to gather the kids when the doorbell rang.

Chapter Fourteen

"Who's here?" Sam asked, narrowing her eyes at Virginia. "You can no longer be trusted, obviously."

"I resent that," her best friend began before meeting her gaze. "And, well, I knew you'd come around, and you did! So, I invited Jordan and told her you wanted her here."

"Why are you like this?" Sam hissed at her over the tabletop as Ben led a gorgeously dressed Jordan into the room. She was wearing a casual plum colored suit over a billowing cream colored top. There were thick gold bands around five of her fingers and her gold pomegranate chain slid against her shirt as she walked. Her fade had recently been trimmed. *So, here I am weeping over the end of things,* Sam thought, *and she goes and gets a haircut.*

"Hi, Virginia, good to see you again." Jordan smiled warmly at the hostess before turning sad, questioning eyes in Sam's direction. "Sam."

"Jordan." Sam's voice came out colder than she'd intended and she saw the butch woman flinch.

Ben came back into the room with a vase of daffodils and placed them between Virginia and Sam, "Jordan brought these! Here, sweetheart. And Jordan, you can sit right next to Sam."

The girls came careening into the room both singing off key a made-up song about the princess made of matzo.

"Girls, this is Sam's friend Jordan. Jordan, this is Gabi and Yael is the one with a bandaid on her forehead. She decided to try to be a trapeze walker using the back of our sofa this morning."

"Nice to meet you, Gabi and Yael." Jordan said sweetly as she sank into the seat next to Sam.

"Hi, Jordan! Mom, we're ready for the seder. Yael wants to sing *Dayenu* at the beginning this time." Gabi flounced into her seat waving a quick hello at Jordan using the plastic pink scepter she'd taken to carrying around.

"Well, you two can wait to sing that until the time is right. Ben, want to start us off, honey?" Virginia rubbed a hand affectionately over her husband's arm and everyone opened their kid-friendly haggadot.

* * *

When it came time to hide the afikomen, Virginia handed it to Sam. "Here, go hide it somewhere good. The girls are great at finding things."

"I'm a champion detective," Yael sang operatically to the room. Sam laughed and took the wrapped up matzo out of the room, sneaking a confused look at Jordan as she turned the corner. The woman was in rapt conversation with the twins about their favorite detective. Sam sighed and went off to find a good hiding spot.

She was pulling her hand out from under the mattress of the guest room when she heard footsteps behind her. Standing up from a crouch, she turned to find herself face to face with Jordan, a closed door behind her.

"Hi," Sam managed.

"Hi," Jordan said, shoving her hands into her pockets.

"So, look—" Sam tried, but then nothing else came out. Instead she felt paralyzed by a lump in her throat.

"Virginia said you wanted her to invite me," Jordan said, sad eyes on Sam's own. "I knew that probably wasn't true, but I couldn't pass up what might be my last shot."

"I do want you here." Her voice came out steadier than she'd imagined.

"You do?" A look of hope splashed across the taller woman's face.

Sam took a step closer and pulled Jordan's hands out of her pockets. She rubbed her thumbs over the knuckles, and raised one of them to her mouth to kiss the back of her hand.

"I do. I'm afraid, Jordan." She took a breath to steady herself. "This is going too fast."

"It is going fast," Jordan agreed, squeezing her hands. "But it doesn't feel like we're rushing it."

"You're right, it feels natural."

"So, shouldn't we listen to that?"

Sam felt her chest glow with the joy caused by just being close to Jordan. She felt the fear too, the fear of being left, of being someone's second choice, but she knew this woman could help her be brave. She stepped closer, into Jordan's arms, into her kiss.

"Listen to your heart!" The words came in as a song from the hallway, muffled by the door, as her best friend meddled for a third time in their relationship. She smiled against Jordan's mouth and they made out for a time as Virginia serenaded them with the Roxette lyrics. "Listen to your heart, when she's calling for you!"

A Year Later

"Yes, definitely, I'll remember it all," Sam lied to Jordan's mother.

It was a chilly, sun-drenched day in Baltimore. Nowruz was a few days behind them. The vibrant celebration had been a crash course in not just Persian culture for Sam but an immersive introduction to Jordan's family. Now Sam was in the kitchen serving as sous chef for Jordan's mother, Mrs. Massachi, a warm woman who hugged Sam multiple times a day and always smelled like oranges and cloves. The older woman was teaching her numerous recipes all at once. Sam had given up committing any of it to memory.

"I'll text it all to Jordan." Mrs. Massachi chuckled as she quickly chopped a mountain of herbs.

They were preparing to host Jordan's three siblings, their partners and children, as well as several cousins, for all of Passover after spending Nowruz at an auntie's house. Sam's brother and his wife were driving in from North Carolina to join in as well, which thrilled her.

Sam tried not to look too relieved at being let off the hook for learning all of the complex combinations of ingredients.

Instead, she reminded herself what a good decision she'd made in coming to Baltimore. She'd taken two weeks off of work to wrap herself in the loving Massachi household after Jordan had read aloud a series of endearing and guilt-inducing texts from her mother.

However, Passover's arrival was bittersweet this year—she was thrilled to celebrate a year of surprising bliss with Jordan. Still, the end of the holiday would mean they had to head back to their own lives and work and not live forever in this delightful family home. She would be glad to be back in a larger bed, though. Jordan and she had shoved two twins together in the childhood bedroom she'd shared with her sister, but it wasn't the same as a real grown-up bed.

Jordan came out behind her and wrapped her arms around her waist, resting her head on her shoulder.

"Should we tell her now?" Jordan's whisper tickled the peach fuzz of Sam's ear, and she shivered all over. Though Jordan had reassured her many times that the walls were pretty thick in the home, she couldn't bring herself to do more than a relatively chaste peck each night. The thought of her future-in-laws hearing them...*involved* was too much for her. *Well, that's really a reason to look forward to leaving, isn't it?*

And thinking of 'future-in-laws,' she turned in Jordan's embrace to glance at Mrs. Massachi's back. "Do you think it's a good time?"

"We should tell her before the rest of the family gets here. Otherwise, she'll accuse us of hiding things."

"What are you two lovebirds whispering about over there? You sound like schoolgirls, giggling and pssh pssh pssh." Jordan's mother turned, flipping her kitchen towel over her shoulder and putting her hands on her hips. "What am I being left out of, hmm?"

The aforementioned lovebirds looked at each other out of

the corners of their eyes, burst out laughing, and Sam knew her face had gone tomato red.

"Well, mom, we have some news." Jordan laced her fingers with Sam's, catching her eye again before turning back to her mother. "We're getting married."

The older woman stood totally still for enough seconds that Sam worried she hadn't heard or was unhappy, but too polite to admit it. Then, she blinked twice, and massive tears rolled down her beautiful, lined face as she swung her arms out to catch them in a hug.

"Oh, my beautiful child has finally found her right person. This is a real match."

Sam missed many of her soon-to-be mother-in-law's exclamations as the woman alternated kissing her cheek, Jordan's cheek, exclaiming in some combination of Farsi, Hebrew, and English, and pulling them in for hug after hug. Sam caught Jordan's eye over her mother's shoulder during one of the hugs. The look on her partner's face was the perfect combination of sheepish and ecstatic. Sam reached out and wrapped her arms around both of the other women and pulled them in as tightly as she could.

So, this is what forever feels like.

THE END

Want more Sam and Jordan?

Sign up for Roz's newsletter and receive a steamy bonus epilogue, "Mimouna Match."

Visit https://signup.rozalexander.com to join the fun!

Acknowledgments

To my partner, who thinks my obsessions are charming.

To my best pals, who try to judge me only fairly.

To my grandmother, who put the first romance novel in my hands at an impressionable age and told me to "skip the naughty bits." I'm not at all sorry to say I did nothing of the sort.

Read them in any order. They share a universe and you'll see your favorite characters in the background of the other stories.

Higher: A Butch-for-Butch Rosh Hashanah Romance

Where do dreams go to wait?

Tali Blue is definitely going back to finish her last semester of rabbinical school...eventually. When she moved back to her hometown seven years ago to help her grandparents raise her younger sisters, she planned on it being temporary. Now though, she has a stable job and a stable life surrounded by the people she's known forever. It's all just fine—and then there's the incredibly annoying surprise of Maple.

Maple never meant to be successful. She just wanted to make weird art and practice her Ladino. And just like that, 15 years of adulthood has built a solid career, a great reputation as an art instructor, and a lackluster love life. It doesn't help that she's strictly a butch-for-butch lesbian. And then comes a sex goddess in the form of short, chunky, smoking hot, and incredibly nervous, butch, Tali Blue.

When Tali's love of family, Maple's art ambitions, and a Rosh Hashanah effort to #savethebees force these two together, both of them may learn that the only way out is up, together. This new year the honey is dripping on a lot more than apples. *Higher* is a steamy, butch for butch, grump-sunshine lesbian romance about what happens when you choose to take your dreams higher.

* * *

A Masc for Purim: A Sapphic Second-Chance Romance

Does true love have an expiration date? What about forgiveness?

Every year, tomboy-femme Liza plans the perfect party for Purim, and every year she goes alone. She's convinced her role as holiday host is enough to find happiness, but lately, the nights have gotten lonelier.

Carrie, a.k.a. Liza's first love, a.k.a. the butch who broke her heart into a million pieces, is back in town and determined to win Liza back. Carrie has spent the last ten years unlearning the internalized ableism that reared its head after her diagnosis of progressive vision loss.

And ten years of regretting leaving Liza.

Their inexperience and inability to be vulnerable with one another may have driven them apart the first time, but has the last decade taught them both to be brave? Luckily, they have the whole megillah to figure it out.

A Masc for Purim is an angsty, steamy, second chance romance novella between a bisexual butch and her tomboy lesbian.

* * *

A Year of Firsts: A Sapphic Toaster Oven Romance

Two people on a journey of self-discovery + a to-do list of 18 experiences = a surprising love story.

CJ has always known what they want out of life: to be a loud, proud queer, to be a part of a community, and to adopt as many puppies as they're legally allowed to own. So far, they're one for three.

In order to answer some of the biggest questions hanging over them, they're paired together with quiet classmate Mia to create a list of 18 experiences to have over the next year.

Mia started considering Judaism for her husband, but a year after their painful divorce she realizes she still wants to explore Jewish community for herself. Her only problem is keeping all the information in her head during her dyspraxia flare-ups.

One year to figure out who they each want to be...and who they want to love. CJ and Mia realize some questions come with surprising answers.

A Year of Firsts is a sapphic (nonbinary + queer woman), "toaster oven," romance about learning to trust yourself.

A child of multiple diasporas, Roz (they/them) has always been obsessed with the idea of home being how you love another person. Their books focus on that idea while showcasing characters of many intersections of identities—plus a little humor, a heavy pour of steam, and a dash of angst.

They are a physically/progressively disabled, white, trans person with ADHD and have more interests than time in the day. You can find them spoiling their three terrible cat-beasts; connecting to their Jewish culture through moon-worship, plantcraft, and cooking traditions; and making weird art when they're not writing or stewarding a native pollinator garden with their beshert.

Stay in touch, sign up for their newsletter: https://signup.rozalexander.com